DANG
LOS

Jean C. Joachim
Ben Tanner

Sensual Romance

Secret Cravings Publishing
www.secretcravingspublishing.com

A Secret Cravings Publishing Book
Sensual Romance

Dangerous Love Lost & Found
Copyright © 2014 Jean C. Joachim & Ben Tanner
Print ISBN: 978-1-63105-495-2

First E-book Publication: October 2014
First Print Publication: January 2015

Cover design by Dawné Dominique
Edited by Tabitha Bower
Proofread by Renee Waring
All cover art and logo copyright © 2014 by Secret Cravings Publishing

ALL RIGHTS RESERVED: This literary work may not be reproduced or transmitted in any form or by any means, including electronic or photographic reproduction, in whole or in part, without express written permission.

All characters and events in this book are fictitious. Any resemblance to actual persons living or dead is strictly coincidental.

PUBLISHER
Secret Cravings Publishing
www.secretcravingspublishing.com

Dedication

I'd like to dedicate this book to all the brave men and women in our Armed Forces who risk their lives for our freedom.

I would like to acknowledge the help and support of the following people:
Ben Tanner, Marilyn Lee, Tabitha Bower, Renee Waring, Beth Walker, Sandy Sullivan,
Ariana Gaynor, Larry Joachim, Elaine Raco Chase, JJ's Book Buddies, and Homer, the pug.

Jean C. Joachim

I would like to thank, first and foremost, my coauthor Jean in giving me this wonderful opportunity to write this series with her. It has been a fun and rewarding project and I appreciate her taking a chance and writing with me. Secondly, I want to thank my wife for being patient with me as it took a lot of my time from her while I plotted, planned, and penned. Thirdly, I want to thank my family and friends for being supportive of me throughout the years. Last, but definitely not least, I would like to thank all the men and women of our armed forces who served and are serving. A lot of times, it is a lonely thankless job, but there are many of us who truly appreciate what you sacrifice to keep us safe daily.
I wish I were still there with you.

Tanner, Ben
USMC Ret.

DANGEROUS LOVE LOST & FOUND
Book 2

Jean C. Joachim
Ben Tanner

Chapter One

New Year's Eve, New York City

Eden pushed through the door of the apartment, almost knocking over someone on the other side.

"Hey, watch it," came a deep voice.

"Sorry," she called out over the loud music.

Pulling the door out of the way, she looked up into a pair of intense, sky blue eyes. The annoyed expression on the man's face softened as his gaze traveled down her body. Hers roamed over his blond crew cut back to his inquisitive eyes and then lower to his crisp uniform and impressive display of medals on a broad chest.

A Marine. Brass. She grinned as she looked him over. *Shoulders as wide as the island of Manhattan. Nice.*

The man extended his hand. "Major Tom Davis."

"Eden Wyatt." *CIA, but that's none of your business.*

"No coat. You live in the building?"

"One flight down."

"Happy New Year, Eden." His smile was warm as it lit up his handsome face.

Hell yes—it is now. "Happy New Year, major. Do they have anything good to drink? I'm thirsty as hell."

"Follow me," he said, taking her by the elbow.

A tiny shiver ran up her arm at the touch of his warm, dry hand. He led her to a small bar set up in the bedroom.

"What's your pleasure—beer, vodka, or wine?" he asked, holding a bottle of vodka in one hand and a beer in the other.

You, honey, on a silver platter. She choked on her saliva for a second, avoiding his gaze. "Vodka. What's there to mix?"

He checked the label of each container. "Tonic, bitter lemon, and orange juice."

"Tonic's good."

He mixed the drink and handed it to her. She flipped her long, blonde hair over her shoulder before taking the glass from him. When their fingers touched, a tingle pricked at her fingertips, almost causing her to drop it.

"Hey." Tom supported the tumbler from the bottom before it toppled to the ground.

"Thanks."

"A little shaky…is this your first drink of the night?"

She nodded. *And you can be my first Marine.* Her gaze lingered on his lips for a second as she wondered what they'd feel like pressed against her own.

"Tara's mom told me about you." Tom leaned against the wall.

"Oh? And what did she tell you?" Eden cocked an eyebrow.

"She asked me if I liked blondes."

"And do you?" She looked up from under her lashes.

"If they look like you? Hell, yeah." He chuckled, his gaze lingering a second too long on her chest.

"Claire Mason is such a matchmaker." Eden shook her head.

"I thought she sold this place," Tom said, looking around.

"She tried, but the buyer couldn't get a mortgage. So, she sold it for practically nothing to Mick and Tara."

"Everyone should have a mom like that."

"Wish I did." Her wistful tone brought his attention back to her. He stepped nearer as Tara and her husband, Mick, entered the room.

"There you are," Tara called to Tom. "Eden. You got here. I'm so glad." She hugged the other woman. "Have you two met?" A little spark lit in Tara's eyes.

Eden nodded.

"Mick's been calling all over town, and it seems all the hotels are booked, Tom," Tara said.

"That's all right. I'll sleep on the subway or something."

"You need a place to stay?" Eden asked, raising her eyebrows.

He nodded.

"My sofa pulls out. You're welcome to bunk in with me," she offered.

His eyes widened a little as a grin spread across his face. "An offer I can't refuse." Again, Tom's gaze traveled the length of her, from the top of her head to the painted toes peeking out from her gold sandals. The heat from his stare almost burned her skin.

"I mean in the living room." She sensed a blush rising in her face.

"Of course," he replied.

Eden noticed Tara and Mick exchanging glances. *They planned this. Damn.* She burst out laughing. "Tara, you're about as subtle as…as…an avalanche."

Tara's cheeks colored. She buried her face in Mick's neck.

"Is this a set up?" the major asked.

"I think so. Look at her," Eden said, pointing to Tara, whose face was as red as a tomato.

"He needed a place to stay. You have a sofa bed…what's wrong with that?" Tara attempted to sound innocent.

"Are you married, major?" Eden asked.

"No, ma'am. Are you?"

She shook her head before turning to stare pointedly at Tara.

"I think I hear someone calling me." Tara took Mick's hand and dragged him out of the room with her. Mick laughed as he followed his wife.

Major Davis poured himself a vodka and tonic. The awkward silence between them grew until he finally broke it. "If you'd rather not have me on your sofa, I understand completely."

"It's fine. Really. You're welcome to stay. I can handle myself, so if you end up sleep walking into my room, be aware that I'm an expert at self-defense." She shot a bold, confident smile at him.

Davis burst out laughing. "No need to worry about me. I'm a sound sleeper, and I never enter a lady's bedroom uninvited."

An engraved invitation or simply a wink? "As long as we're clear on the ground rules," Eden said, taking a swig of her drink.

"Very clear, ma'am."

They moseyed out into the living room. The lights were low and candles burned on the mantle. The party was small, perhaps ten people. Slow music played "How Do You Fall in Love" by Alabama.

"Care to dance?" Tom asked her, setting his glass on the mantle.

A shy smile crept over her face as she placed hers on a side table. "Love to."

The major took her hand in his and led her out to the center of the room. He placed his other hand on her waist and pulled her a little closer. Eden folded her fingers over his shoulder and stepped into his embrace. "How Do You Fall in Love" blended into "Far Away" by Nickelback, and they kept dancing.

For the second song, Tom pulled her in closer. Eden rested her head on his shoulder. Her soft chest flattened a little against his hard muscle. The pressure of their bodies touching warmed her blood. A whiff of his aftershave mixed with the smell of his freshly ironed shirt and his unique scent, intoxicating her. Although her mind willed her to move back from his seductive warmth, her body rebelled, softening against him.

He was an expert dancer, guiding her effortlessly around the room, keeping time to the music. When his embrace became more intimate as the song continued, she closed her eyes. Never disrespectful, the way he held her excited her and imparted a sense of safety at the same time. His grip was firm and sexy. The sensation was heady.

She shook her head once. *You're never safe. Stop it. Be alert. Don't forget.* Her eyes popped open, she snapped to attention, and her body stiffened.

He bent to whisper in her ear. "Everything okay?"

He could feel me change. We're dancing too close. But she didn't want to move away. *If I keep my eyes open, I'll be okay. Breathe.* Her muscles loosened, and her body relaxed again. *Alert doesn't mean tense.*

Finally, the song changed to a fast dance. They separated and finished their drinks. Eden motioned him to the kitchen. There were platters of finger foods, crudités, cheese cubes, olives, pigs in blankets, and chocolate covered strawberries.

"Another vodka and tonic?" he asked.

"Sure."

Tom took their glasses into the bedroom for refills. Eden filled a plate to overflowing with hors d'oeuvres. She met him in the small dining area. They pulled chairs up to the tall window and gazed out at the city lights.

Tom raised his tumbler to hers. "To a great new year." He moved his seat closer to hers.

She clinked her glass against his and smiled. They each took a sip. Eden placed hers on the windowsill so she could pick up a cube of cheese and hold it to his mouth. He ate it slowly, holding her gaze with his. He picked up a strawberry and held it to her lips. She munched on it, keeping eye contact. The air between them crackled with electricity. *He's so tall...handsome.*

They fed each other back and forth until she drew the tip of his finger into her mouth. She licked strawberry juice off it then pushed it slowly out again. Looking up, she saw desire flicker in his eyes and a flush steal into his cheeks. *Gotcha.* Eden noticed his gaze drop to her mouth, so she swiped the tip of her tongue across her lower lip. Sweat broke out on his forehead as he stared.

They were sitting close, knees touching when everyone started yelling. Fireworks were heard in the distance. *Midnight.*

He whispered so softly she almost didn't hear him. "If you're going to do that...I'm going to do this." He leaned over and brushed his lips against hers then planted a real kiss. When he sat back, he said, "Happy New Year, Eden."

She was breathless and could only nod her head.

* * * *

He couldn't believe the heat coursing through him from the brush of her knee with his. Holding her when they danced had been a turn on and feeding her had stoked the fire. Their kiss made him want more. *Slow down, Tom. You just met her, and you're moving in. She's wary. Back off. But damn, she smells so good.*

"What's that perfume you're wearing?"

"Lilac."

"Makes me think of spring." He spread his arm across the back of her chair.

"Lilacs are a spring flower. My favorite, in fact. Like it?"

Like it? It's driving me wild. "Could say that." He grinned at her.

"That's what true love looks like," she said, motioning toward the corner of the room. Tara and Mick stood in semi-darkness, locked in a passionate embrace.

He chuckled. "They're a devoted pair. Never seen a love so fast or intense as theirs."

She turned to face him. "Have you ever experienced true love?"

"I'm still waiting for Cupid to bring his arrow to my bunk." *Maybe you'll be my first.*

She laughed.

"You?" he asked.

Her smile melted away. "Once."

He raised an eyebrow. "Oh?"

"He died." She paused. "I don't want to talk about it." She lowered her lashes.

"I'm so sorry," he said, taking her small hand in his. "Were you married?"

She shook her head, her eyes glistening with unshed tears.

Idiot. She said she didn't want to talk about it.

He snaked his arm around her shoulders and drew her into his embrace. She shuddered then sighed. Her hair tickled his nose, and her scent grew stronger.

The sound of someone clearing their throat caused them to split apart. She turned her face away from him, but he could see her wipe her eyes.

"Happy New Year," Tara chirped.

"Happy New Year," Tom echoed, pushing to his feet.

He and Mick shook hands. Eden embraced Tara.

"So, I guess you're okay with the major bunking in with you?" Tara asked.

"Fine."

Tom noticed people had begun leaving. *Gotta give the newlyweds some time alone.* He stretched and stifled a yawn. "I'm an early riser. Time to hit the rack."

Eden picked up her purse while Tom retrieved his duffle bag and hoisted the strap over his shoulder.

"Lead on, pretty lady."

As they headed toward the hall stairs, Tom glanced back. Wearing a shy smile, Mick stood behind Tara with an arm around her middle. Resting one hand on Mick's arm, she leaned back against him and raised her other one to wave. *Damn, he's lucky.*

Eden slipped down the narrow stairwell easily while Tom had to maneuver his bulky duffle this way and that to keep from bumping the walls.

She reached the landing before him. She stopped to unlatch three locks then crouched down. While her hand turned the knob slowly, her gaze zeroed in on the bottom, near the sill.

Tom stood by, fascinated. As she opened it, something fell out onto the floor. She picked it up. *A match. Why does she have a match stuck in the jamb?*

Once they were inside, she shut the door immediately and secured all three locks again. He shot her a questioning glance. *Three locks?*

"Wondering why I do that, aren't you? I had a…home invasion. Was attacked. Now, I put a match in so I know if there's someone in the apartment. Keeps me sane."

"Clever. Is that why you learned self-defense?"

"You could say that," she said, placing her purse on the coffee table. "Long story."

"A woman of mystery…"

Don't go there," she warned. "How about a nice glass of brandy to top off the evening?"

What doesn't she want me to know? Now, I've gotta find out. "Sure." He looked around at the apartment for a place where his bag would be out of the way.

The living room was small, but nicely designed. High ceilings gave an airy feeling to the little apartment. Cream-colored walls had a few beautiful oil paintings of country scenes. The sofa was covered in dark green velvet. A small bookcase in oak matched the coffee table. The space had a serene feeling to it. Tom was comfortable right away.

Eden disappeared into the tiny kitchen.

"Can I help?" he called after her.

"Nope. Thanks. Got it." She returned carrying a silver tray holding a crystal decanter half filled with brandy and two small snifters. She set it down on the coffee table.

Filling the small glasses halfway, she handed one to Tom and sat back next to him on the couch, raising hers to her lips.

He took a swig. "This is fine."

"Thanks. Best I could afford."

"You work?" he asked, shifting to get more comfortable and face her.

"I'm unemployed right now. I've been a travel agent, a cake baker…" She sipped her brandy.

He raised an eyebrow. *Self-defense expert, a bit paranoid, and no permanent job? Doesn't add up.*

"What are you doing in New York? I hope not chasing down a terrorist threat."

"Mick's an old buddy of mine—elementary, middle, and high school then college, and finally, the Marines. I'm visiting the newlyweds before I report to Washington in two days. Then back here for a couple more before I head back."

"Were you in the Middle East?" She refilled Tom's glass.

"Afghanistan."

"Can't talk about it, right?" She smiled.

"Right." He swirled the liquid around in his mouth for a second before swallowing.

"Did you like it there?"

"I wouldn't say I liked it. It was an assignment, and we were successful. Guess I liked the result. Living there is hell." *Lots of questions. Why?*

"I'm sorry. Can you tell me where you're going?" She crossed her legs.

"I'm afraid I can't." He studied her face to pick up her reaction to his words. *Why does she want to know?*

"Must be hard to have a relationship with so much secrecy."

"If you were my wife, I could tell you. Maybe not everything, but a helluva lot more. But you'd never repeat it because it might threaten my safety."

"Still. Has to make it hard to be married, if your wife isn't in the service, too." Eden took a sip of brandy.

"That's why I haven't had a visit from Cupid yet." Tom chuckled.

"Looking for a woman who can put up with that, eh?" She leaned back against a cushion and rested her arm on the sofa back.

"Bingo." *I wish you were military.*

"You might be surprised at how much a...woman like me...can understand." She shot him a flirtatious glance.

"Maybe you're different..." He leaned in a bit closer.

"What do you mean?" Her eyes widened.

"Something about you...doesn't add up."

Eden pushed to her feet and began pacing. "Why do you say that? Can't I enjoy making cakes and traveling?"

"No problem. It's okay. I like you the way you are." *That set her off. Must be on the right track. I need to know what she's hiding. I'll bide my time.*

She stopped, lifted the decanter, and offered him more brandy. *No more to drink until I know who she really is.* He put his hand over the glass and shook his head. "That's plenty for me. Thanks. Time to turn in."

He stood up. She opened the sofa, retrieved a set of sheets from a drawer, and then retired to her room. He made up the bed then undressed. When he was down to his pants and socks, her door opened. She came out wearing a short, black jersey gown with slim straps. There was a tiny, white bow between her breasts. Unable to stop himself, Tom let out a low whistle. She turned, startled.

"Didn't mean to scare you but, wow, Eden. Do you always dress like that for bed?"

She smiled warmly at him as she moved closer. "Not usually."

"Didn't think so," he said smugly as he folded his shirt.

"Usually, I sleep naked."

Tom gulped and coughed, choking for a moment on his own saliva.

"You asked."

Chapter Two

Eden pulled up the covers and turned out the light.
"Night, Davis," she called out.
"Night, Eden."
She slipped her hand under her pillow. When it made contact with the cold metal of a gun barrel, she relaxed and smiled. *It's there. I'm good.* Closing her eyes, Eden hoped, in vain, for a peaceful rest. Nightmares plagued her. Tossing and turning, she ripped the sheets up off the bed. In her dreams, there he was, plain as day.

Eden backed up until she came to a wall. Fadi kept coming.
"Take your clothes off," he demanded.
She shook her head.
"I said take your clothes off. Do it. Now!"
Eden thought for a moment. There were six armed guards with AK-47s. And Fadi. If she defended herself, he would know she was a spy. Then, they would execute her like they did Jerry. She had to keep her cover or die. Slowly, with shaking hands, she began to undress.
Fadi licked his lips and stared at her. "Faster! I haven't got all day."
She fumbled with buttons, biding time, her mind working furiously, trying to find a plan, an escape, a way out.
"I'll give you thirty seconds to strip, or I'll do it myself, with this." He pulled out a Janbiya, with a blade seven inches long.
Eden gulped. She sped up and soon was standing naked in front of him, shivering, though the heat in the room was suffocating. He approached her, violating her first with his leering stare. Pushing up against her, he reached into his pants. Fortunately, he wasn't fully erect. He shoved his hand down between her legs.
"Ah, already wet for me. You're such a whore. You don't care who gives it to you, do you?" An ugly smile raised his lips.
When he withdrew his hand, it was covered in blood. He screamed a curse and jumped back from her. "You disgusting

bitch! You're bleeding, and you didn't tell me." He slapped her across the face.

The pain in her jaw kept her from smiling. *Never been so glad to get a surprise period as today,* she thought. A shuddering sigh shot through her body.

Fadi picked up her shirt and wiped off his hand. *"Wear this...this filthy blood. Show the world what a pig you are. I'm not finished with you. You can't bleed forever, bitch. And I'll be back. I'll be back to take what's mine."*

Asleep in her bed, Eden began to shake and cry. She awoke gulping for air as a scream escaped her throat. The room was pitch black. She was awake, but the trembling continued.

There was a figure outlined in black at the door. Eden reached under her pillow and pulled out a Glock 39. She aimed and fired, but her hand was shaking so badly she missed by a mile. The figure dove for the floor.

"It's me, Tom. Eden, don't shoot."

She heard the words, but they were jumbled together. She couldn't make sense of them as she tried to steady the gun in her hand. The man leapt up, grabbed her wrist hard with one hand, and dislodged the firearm with the other. He put it on the ground and kicked it under the bed.

Eden still didn't know who he was. Cowering, she sobbed, "Don't...don't hurt me...please...don't..."

He pulled her into his arms, holding her tightly, stroking her hair. "It's Tom Davis. Eden, you're okay. You were dreaming."

The warmth of his body brought her back to the present. She hugged him tightly and let out a deep, shuddering breath. He kissed her hair. When her eyes adjusted to the darkness, lightened only by a few moonbeams, she gazed into his.

"You're all right, honey," he murmured, cupping her cheek.

"Davis? Tom?" The strap on her gown had fallen halfway down her arm, and her hair was matted down.

"It's me." He wiped a tear on her cheek with his thumb.

"Thank God." She clung to him for a few more moments before she realized he was bare-chested. She slid her hands down slowly until they came into contact with a waistband. *Boxers.*

A deep breath filled her nostrils with his delicious, masculine scent mixed with a touch of Jovan Musk aftershave. Her fingers dug into the muscles of his back as she relaxed against him. *He's a big man.* The sense of safety he had imparted to her during their slow dance returned.

He loosened his grip slightly.

"Please, don't go," she whispered, her breathing back to normal again.

His fingers fanned out on her back, pressing her closer. Eden snuggled into him, closing her eyes for only a moment. *So good to relax.* She kissed his pecs once, opened her eyes again, leaned back, and peered up at him.

"Do you have dreams like this often?" His brows knit, his face serious.

"This is my most frequent one. I have others, sometimes." She moved back a bit.

"What happened to you? You have serious nightmares, you rig your front door, keep a gun under your pillow, and you're a self-defense expert. Who are you, Eden?" Tom let go and stepped away a fraction.

"Didn't fool you for long, did I? I'm with the State Department." She sat back on her haunches.

"CIA?"

"I can't tell you."

"What can you tell me?" A flicker of something in his eyes held her attention.

"Not much. I had a…uh…bad…experience in Lebanon two years ago. Can't seem to shake it." She chewed her thumb.

"It takes time."

"Two years…you'd think…" Her voice trailed off. She pulled up the strap of her gown.

"Hey, you didn't have to do that on my account." He smirked.

"Enjoying the view?" She cocked an eyebrow at him.

"Could say that. You okay now?"

"Sure. Fine." *Why did you let me go?*

Even through dim light, Eden could see desire glitter in his eyes. He closed the gap between them again, gripping her upper arms and pulling her to him. He lowered his mouth to hers in a tentative kiss.

God I want him…not yet. Too soon. With her hand on his neck, she held him still while she deepened the kiss.

He reacted immediately, pulling her flush up against him, crushing her breasts into his chest. One hand cradled her head while the other slid down to her hip. Her resolve to resist began to melt away under the seductive caresses of his lips and tongue. His passion took her breath away, dissolving some of the chill surrounding her heart.

Before her self-control vanished completely, rational thinking took over. Pushing away from him, she took a deep breath and moved back.

"Sorry. Got a bit carried away. You're a beautiful woman and dressed—or should I say undressed?—like that, well, you're irresistible."

The wall of polite conversation fell back into place. "Here are my rules—no commitment and no one-night stands. Short term only."

"Why? I don't mean the one-night stands. I get that. I mean the no commitment."

"I'm not safe. I can't tell you why. I don't want anything bad to happen to you."

"I can take care of myself. I'm not exactly defenseless." He chuckled.

"This is different. I don't want to talk about it. Can you live with those rules?"

"The no-one-night-stand thing is fine. But the no commitment…we'll see."

She chuckled. "You're a stubborn, independent kinda guy, eh?"

"I'm used to making the rules, but I bend them a little, sometimes."

"So, I should be taking orders from you?" She raised her eyebrows. "Don't think so. Majors make the rules, huh? What makes you think you can control me?" She crossed her arms over her breasts.

"You might be the one. And if you are, no silly rules are going to stand in my way."

She laughed. "Silly rules? You've got some nerve." She grabbed the extra pillow on her bed and bashed his chest with it. The second swing at him wasn't so successful. He caught her wrist with one hand while yanking the pillow out of her grip with the other.

Before she could take a breath, he had them trapped over her head, clamped together in one of his big hands. His other held her chin while his body, resting on his elbow, lightly brushed against hers.

"I could get out of this if I wanted to, you know."

He challenged her with mirth in his eyes. "Go ahead. I dare you."

"Who says I want to?" She shot him a seductive smile and arched her back, pressing her breasts into him.

"Nope. No one-night stands," he said, sitting up and freeing her hands. "That's a rule."

"Why you…" An expression of mock anger washed over her face.

He laughed. "Your rules, beautiful. I'm only obeying orders."

She chuckled with him.

He rose from the bed. "Are you all right to get back to sleep?"

"I think so. Thanks…for everything." *I wish he'd stay. He'd get the wrong idea…but I could sleep so well tucked safely into those big arms.* She sighed.

"It was my pleasure." He fished the gun out from under the bed before he moved toward the door with a laconic gait, taking his time.

Her gaze followed his body, studying the width of his shoulders before slipping all the way down the muscles in his back to his butt. *Pretty cute.*

He stopped, tucked the Glock in his waistband, and turned, filling up the doorway.

"Hey! That's my gun."

"Not for tonight. I'll keep it. You'll be safe with me here."

She smiled. "Yeah, but who'll keep me safe from you?"

He cocked an eyebrow at her. "You're sure you're okay…you don't need me to stay?" A small smile curled his lips.

Don't tempt me. "Is that an offer?"

He blushed. "I didn't mean…"

"Yes, you did. Are you trying to seduce me?" She tried to stifle a grin.

"No, no…making sure you're okay…secure and all." His gaze avoided hers.

"If you want me to feel totally safe, give me back my gun."

"I'm keeping the firearm." He patted his waist.

"Don't trust me?"

"Not for a second." He laughed.

"Right you are, too." She flashed a flirtatious look his way.

"Goodnight, Eden. I'm here if you need me."

"Goodnight, major. I'll remember that if I get…lonely."

He chuckled as he shut the door behind him.

Eden snuggled down in her bed, clutching a spare pillow to her chest. *Wow, he's amazing. It's warm in here.* She kicked off the covers then tried a few different positions before falling asleep.

* * * *

Tom put the gun on the small table next to the sofa before he climbed back in bed. He lay still, staring at the ceiling, trying to take in what had happened. *I got shot at by a crazed, beautiful woman who may be a secret agent. And I thought this would be a quiet little side trip. Hah! She's amazing. Fiery, gorgeous, sexy as hell. But, her rules. I've gotta know more about her. Her teasing is driving me wild, but I'll be damned if I stop until I get her into bed.*

He closed his eyes, but visions of Eden taking off her clothes filled his mind. Finally, he fell into a restless slumber.

The sun woke him up when it poked through a crack in the heavy, dark curtains at six thirty. In a couple of seconds, he had his bearings, stretched his legs, and yawned. A smile spread across his face when he remembered Eden in her little, black nightie. He hoped she'd parade by in it again. He laced his fingers behind his head while his gaze spanned the room. His military training was so ingrained that he automatically checked out anyplace he stayed.

One door, windows locked, second floor, facing the street, unlikely for break-in. Any more weapons here? He didn't believe someone as prepared or as paranoid as Eden would be satisfied with only one gun in the house. He spied a closet and considered exploring it while she slept. *She's Tara's neighbor, not an enemy. Calm down. Besides, she's probably CIA, almost as good as military.*

He rolled on his side and propped up on his elbow. The apartment was neat, but not excessively so. Feminine touches, like a pink fan framed and mounted on the wall and a white, crocheted doily on a small table, made him smile. There was nothing frilly about Eden's personality, yet she was all female.

He heard the bedroom door open. His eyes widened as he spied her tiptoe out of her room. *Damn. My lucky day. The nightie.* He couldn't keep a wide grin off his face as his gaze followed her body, barely clad in the clingy material. *If that were any lower, she'd be topless.* His mouth went dry, and his breathing quickened a bit as he watched her try to steal silently across the floor.

"If you're trying not to wake me, you're too late."

Eden jumped back and gasped. "Scare me to death, why don't you?" She clasped her hand to her throat and turned to look at him.

Her tangled hair hung beautifully around her shoulders. Her mouth, still pink from remnants of last night's lipstick, invited him to kiss her. Her legs were slender and shapely. Tom's groin tightened. He could hardly control himself.

"Is something showing that shouldn't be?" She blushed becomingly while she tugged gently on her nightie.

He shook his head. *Nope. Everything that's showing should be...and more wouldn't hurt.*

"Let me get coffee started. Then, I'll rustle up a couple of eggs."

"Thought I'd take you out to breakfast."

"Aren't you sweet? Mick and Tara are expecting us for brunch at eleven. But that's too long to wait to eat. I doubt anything is open this early on New Year's. How about you take me to dinner tonight instead?"

"Deal." He threw the covers off the bed and swung his legs over the side. "Can I help?"

She shook her head. "Tiny New York City kitchens...no room for two. If you did get in there with me, why, we'd be engaged when you left." She chuckled and tossed him a towel. "Why don't you have first crack at the bathroom? There's only one in a place this size."

"On my way." *Sassy even early in the morning. Think I like that.*

After she entered the kitchen, Tom padded across the room. He discovered that the bathroom was about as tiny as the kitchen. He plastered himself against the sink to get the door closed. The shower stall was barely big enough for him. While he was lathering up to shave, he heard Eden singing. Her voice had a sweet lilt to it, which was surprising considering her sharp tongue. *She's like a diamond with many facets.*

The delicious aroma of bacon cooking crept into the bathroom, seducing his taste buds. His stomach rumbled. As he finished wiping off his face, he realized he had forgotten to bring in his clothes. *Towel around the waist. Give her a gander, like she gave me.* He chuckled at the bold assumption that she was interested in him. *Is she a flirt, or does she like me? Guess I'll find out now.* He gave a short laugh as he opened the door.

"What's so funny—?" she began, but ended in a gasp when she saw him.

"Sorry. Left my clothes out here."

Her gaze slid down his chest like the caress of a warm hand. "Wow. Great way to wake me up, major."

He sensed heat moving up into his neck. Her frank appreciation of his body embarrassed him more than he had expected. They stood, staring at each other, until the pleasant bacon aroma turned slightly acrid.

"The bacon!" she shrieked, returning quickly to the kitchen.

The smoke alarm went off then, sending a shrill scream through the apartment. Tom stood on a small stool and reset it while she pulled the pan off the flame then opened a window. They both burst out laughing.

"If you'd stop running around, undressed like…that…" She gestured with her hand. "I wouldn't burn the bacon. I'm only human, major. Cover up or breakfast'll end up in the garbage."

"Aye, aye," he said, unzipping his duffel to retrieve his clothes. He disappeared into the bathroom and came out outfitted in his dress blues "B" uniform—blue dress coat with ribbons, blue slacks with the red blood stripe, and spit-shined oxford shoes with black socks.

Eden gasped again when she saw him. "You keep getting better," she chuckled.

"Your turn."

"Food first." She set two plates loaded with bacon and eggs down on a tiny, round table in the corner of the room.

Tom squeezed himself into a chair and chowed down. When they finished, Eden went into the bathroom. He made up the bed and folded it back as a sofa, stowing his gear in the duffel. She came out soon after with a towel tucked around her slim frame. He couldn't rip his gaze away from her breasts, in danger of being fully exposed at any second. She scampered through the living room and into her bedroom quickly, shutting the door behind her. Tom laughed.

She popped her head out. "What's so funny?"

"You. Like I'm not going to see you if you're running, bouncing, and wiggling..." He kept chuckling.

Her head disappeared as quickly as it had appeared. Within ten minutes, she returned, completely dressed in snug, boot cut dark blue jeans, black suede boots, a scooped neck cashmere sweater in light blue to match her eyes, and a gold heart pendant that drew his eyes to her cleavage. Her hair was neatly combed, falling loosely a few inches down her back.

"You look fantastic."

"Thank you." She smiled warmly at him. "How about a walk before brunch?"

"Sounds like a plan."

Eden opened the closet and grabbed a light blue, down parka. She slipped a white, knit cap on and zipped up. "It's cold in New York City, especially when you're walking."

Tom put on his trench coat, and opened the front door. Eden donned gloves to match her hat then waltzed out into the hall. He followed. She added a matchstick and fastened the locks.

"I'm here. Do you really need to do that?"

"You've no idea."

He shrugged, and they descended the stairs. It was eight o'clock, and the streets were completely quiet. Tom took her hand as she steered them toward the river. The wind picked up as they approached Riverside Drive.

Despite the cold, the sky was bright blue and the sun cast light but little warmth on the scene. Larger gray or beige buildings stood next to more colorful brick and painted brownstones on the side streets. There were two people, bundled up, walking their dogs, who also wore jackets against the cold, January day.

This was Tom Davis's first trip to New York City. As they hit West End Avenue, he looked up and down, marveling at how many buildings there were. As far as the eye could see, there were apartments, some with awnings and some not. Trees planted in front of the structures were short, bare, spindly, and gray, like fingers of the dead reaching from a grave to the sky.

"Do you like living here?" he asked, his gaze lingering on the small, quirky townhouses and brownstones they passed.

"I do. It's a great place to get lost. So many people."

"Maybe a few too many for me." He frowned.

"You get used to it. I stay to myself much of the time. Mick and Tara are almost my only friends. This is a good city if you want to remain anonymous."

"You don't seem like the type," he said, holding her hand.

"You don't know me very well. You'd be surprised."

"I didn't think you were a city girl."

"I'm not. I adapted. I do what I have to, to survive."

"I get it."

"You're a Marine. I'm sure you understand." She stopped abruptly as the light turned red.

"Completely."

"There are many beautiful things tucked away in this city. I like to walk. You'd be surprised what I find here when I'm out by myself."

"Would I?"

She nodded. "Sniffen Court, a tiny row of townhouses with their own private entrance in the Murray Hill section. A few cobblestone streets with houses over a hundred years old in the Village."

"Sounds quaint."

"There are so many places dripping with charm and history. You have to take the time to see them." The light turned green again, and they continued their way West.

"And do you?"

"I'm a woman with no man—nothing but time on my hands."

"Maybe not anymore. Maybe now you have someone to share them with."

"Maybe I do." She smiled up at him, her sunglasses masking the true expression in her eyes.

"Where are we going?" He spied the river not far away.

"That's the Hudson. It's beautiful. So is Riverside Park, where we're headed. There's even a marina there."

"A marina?"

"Yep. With all sorts of boats, including houseboats. Some people live there all year long. I think they're nuts because it gets so damn cold, but hey…different strokes and all that."

"That I gotta see," Tom said, crossing with her.

They entered the park at 83rd Street and turned left, heading downtown.

"Where are the boats?"

"Patience, Davis. We're coming to them. Just down these stairs."

They took the wide steps quickly. They marched through an open-air restaurant closed for the season, out onto a sidewalk and into the park. Tom smiled when he spied the bobbing boats in the water at the small marina.

"Bet you didn't expect this." She stopped and turned toward him.

"Since I met you, beautiful, my life has become one huge surprise after another."

Chapter Three

The clip clop of Major Davis' dress shoes on the pavement was the only sound. The park isn't deep, but it spans many blocks on the Upper West Side, snaking up the shore of the Hudson. Although it wasn't a numbing cold, the wind whipping off the river made it chilly enough so that the couple's breath was visible in the air. The major tightened his grip on Eden's small hand.

She quickly scanned the vicinity and didn't see anyone who looked threatening, so she turned her attention to him. The bright sunshine melted a thin dusting of snow on tree limbs, causing water to drip and glisten like diamonds. When she looked up at him, the clear, blue sky behind him mirrored the color of his eyes, dazzling her.

The pair stopped when they got to the marina. There were water vessels of all sizes, from motor boats to yachts. Two rectangular houseboats had light peeking through café curtains. Smaller boats were deserted and bounced morosely in the gentle waves of winter. Larger yachts, appearing out of place, barely swayed in the choppy water. Tom mused aloud that he thought they'd be more at home in Florida or the Caribbean.

They gazed at the vessels, commenting on which ones they liked best. Some had colored lights for Christmas still strung around their decks while others remained unadorned and quiet. The sound of water lapping against the sides and the occasional cry of a seagull broke the silence. Eden stepped nearer, and Tom slipped his arm around her shoulders as if by instinct. She cuddled into his embrace.

The waterway was empty except for one, lone tugboat.

"What's on the other side?" he asked, pointing to some posh, low-rise condominiums.

"New Jersey...the Palisades further up." She motioned to a forested area to the right.

"So, the Hudson divides New York from New Jersey?"

"Sort of."

"Must be amazing to live on the river, like they do there," he said, pointing.

"Amazing and expensive."

"Imagine summertime."

"Must be beautiful."

He nodded.

She retreated to a bench, sitting down and rubbing her gloved hands together. She heard a rustle in a bush behind her, but assumed it was a bird. So wrapped up was Eden in the major that she dropped her guard for a moment. Staring at his back while he faced the water, she dreamt of a hot night with him, unaware of the shadowy figure of a man moving closer. Breaking into her reverie, he sprang, grabbing her and thrusting a knife to her neck.

She cried out, and Tom whirled around.

The assailant fastened one arm around her middle, holding her in a vise-like grip. The other hand, shaking slightly, rested the blade against her skin. The stench of tobacco, dirt, and rancid whiskey pouring off him made her retch. The steel was ice cold, giving her chills. It pressed against her sideways, so it wouldn't cut. But Eden knew he could turn it in a heartbeat and her blood would gush out, spilling onto the pavement.

She focused her attention on Davis, controlling her runaway heartbeat with regular breathing.

"Give me your watch and wallet, soldier boy, or I slice her pretty, little throat."

Eden tried to reach behind her with her foot, but the crafty man sidestepped her attempt to take him down. He was six inches taller than she, and when she put her hand on his wrist, he pressed the knife closer, almost breaking the skin.

"Keep going slut and I'll slice you up like a Sunday ham. Stay still or you die right now."

She froze, believing his words.

Tom raised his hand. "Stop! Don't hurt her. I'll give you what you want." He stepped closer as he feigned removing his watch.

"That's close enough, buddy," the man said, gesturing at Tom with the weapon.

The minute the blade left Eden's neck, Tom sprang like a trapdoor spider at the assailant, grabbing his wrist with a bone-crushing grip. He must have squeezed hard, because the man dropped the knife. Eden slumped to the ground, confusing the robber as she fell away from him.

With Eden on the ground, Tom had a clear field to take out the man and started to pummel him. His left fist struck squarely on the assailant's jaw. Tom's second hit was aimed at the solar plexus, taking the man's breath away completely, causing him to collapse. Tom jumped on top of him—left, right, left, right. He kept hitting until the guy was out cold.

The major picked up the weapon, put it in his pocket, and turned to check on Eden. She was lying on the grass, resting on one elbow, smiling at him. "I was taught to 'faint' in situations like that. Then, the person has a dead weight to deal with, throwing him off. It worked."

Tom chuckled. "Very smart." He put out his hand, which she took, and he lifted her to a standing position and into his arms.

Regardless of her bravery, Eden was shaking. "Do you think he was a common, garden-variety mugger or someone else…someone with an agenda, out for revenge?" She snuggled her face into his coat.

"Seems to me like a dumb crook, not a terrorist. Is that what you meant?"

She nodded, but stayed in the safety of his embrace. "Thanks."

When she looked up at him, he kissed her. "You're safe."

Eden's gaze scanned the vicinity again. When she didn't see another soul around, she relaxed against him. The pleasing fragrance of his masculine scent combined with his aftershave soothed her. *I could get used to this. Having him around is…great.* Allowing herself a minute of weakness, Eden closed her eyes for a brief second, sinking into him.

After a few minutes, Tom broke the embrace. He flipped his assailant over and zip tied his hands behind his back. Noticing Eden's raised eyebrows, he spoke,

"We carry them all the time in Afghanistan. It's just habit to slip a few in my pocket."

Eden smiled as he pulled out his phone and called the police. Twenty minutes later, they had given their statements and were on their way to Mick and Tara's.

Tom lifted his hand and glanced at his watch. "When are we supposed to be at Mick and Tara's?" he asked.

Eden pulled his wrist within her view. "In ten minutes. We'd better hustle." She stepped away from him, but slipped her hand in his. They walked quietly, enjoying the stolen moment of silence in such a busy, noisy city. The park was stark with the trees barren and the grass brown, but the sun shone, glistening off the river. *Don't get excited. He's leaving tomorrow. Maybe he'll be back...maybe not. Wouldn't be the first time a guy took off. But while he's here...so nice.*

She took him home via a different side street, so he could see new scenery. They climbed the hill at 79th Street. Huge, double-length crosstown buses lumbered by, behind empty taxicabs. She noticed him taking in his surroundings. He was sharp, no doubting that. *Another item on the plus side for the major.* Even so, she hung back, unwilling to believe her luck had changed.

The lobby of her brownstone was chilly. Still, being out of the biting wind was a relief. A blast of warm air met them when Tara opened the door of the apartment, along with the delicious aroma of cinnamon and Canadian bacon cooking. They were hustled right in and cups of hot, mulled wine were thrust into their hands.

"The hell with hot chocolate. This'll warm you up faster. Major, your ears are quite red. Is that from the cold or Eden's language?" Tara joked.

"This is delicious," Eden said, sipping the steaming liquid slowly.

"The cold. Of course, Eden wouldn't use foul language...she's a lady." Tom's eyes twinkled when Eden broke up.

"I probably know more bad words than you do." She unzipped her jacket.

"Doubt that." He put down the wine, took off his coat, folded Eden's over his, and placed them on the bed.

Mick came out of the kitchen and shook Davis' hand before he led them to a table set for four in the living room. They were soon joined by Tara, who parceled out Eggs Benedict onto each plate. Conversation halted as they dug into the delicious meal.

Halfway through, Tara put down her fork and sat back. "So, major...tell me about Mick. What don't I know...that I should?" She raised an eyebrow at him.

Mick squirmed in his chair.

"I don't know where to begin. There's plenty you don't know, and I'm sure as hell not going to tell you. I like living," Tom said, shooting a grin at his friend.

"Tell us about you, then." Eden changed the subject.

"What do you want to know?"

"Everything...where you were born, siblings, parents...sexual history...the usual..." She snickered.

Tom choked on his wine, coughing, while Eden laughed. Mick got up and pounded his friend on the back. Tara handed him a glass of water.

"Sorry, major. I didn't know I was touching a sore spot there."

"Surprised, that's all. Let's see...I was born in Georgia. My parents are deceased, unfortunately. I have a sister, Jennifer, a year younger..."

"And..." Eden prompted.

Tom leaned over close to her. "As for the rest...I guess you'll have to find out firsthand." He grinned.

Eden burst out laughing. "Did your younger sister ever hang out with you and Mick?"

"Are you kidding? A little sister is like poison...except in high school. Then, she helps you get dates," Tom answered.

Tom and Eden gathered the empty plates and took them into the kitchen before coming back to the table. Tara joined them with a plate loaded with hot cinnamon buns, dripping with white icing. She passed out small plates and each took one of the round confections. Then, seating herself, she cleared her throat while the others dug into the pastry.

"Did your sister ever date Mick?" Tara cast an inquiring eye at Tom first then Mick, who colored.

"Don't think so. Unless there's something he needs to tell me."

"No, no. Never went out with Jen," Mick said, waving his hands back and forth.

"But you wanted to? Is she pretty?" Tara asked.

Mick turned several shades of red.

"I guess that answers my question. Is she married?"

Tom shook his head.

"I see. Where does she live?" Tara sat back in her chair, watching Mick, though she directed her question to the major.

"In Georgia. You don't have to worry about Mick. He's always been a one-woman man, when he had a woman, that is." Tom took a bite of the bun.

"And when he didn't?" Tara cocked an eyebrow at her husband.

"Probably a horndog, just like the rest." Eden put in. "Out to get whatever they can."

"That's a pretty cynical attitude," Tom said, after swallowing his food.

"Realistic. I know men, and that's the way they are until their hearts get involved. And even then, some don't know when to stop."

"And how many men have you known?" The major stared into her eyes.

Eden's smirk morphed into a nervous smile. "Enough."

"Enough? That's not a number," Tom persisted.

"I'm not going there, major. You'll have to guess."

"And you'll tell me if I'm right?"

"Are you crazy?" Her eyes grew wide.

They all laughed, breaking the growing tension. Frowning, Tara pushed to her feet and cleared the dishes. An obviously worried Mick followed her into the kitchen.

"Do you think she's really mad?" Tom asked.

Eden shook her head. "I doubt it. She's so head-over-heels for that guy."

"It must be nice…to have someone love you that much," Tom murmured, looking down at his hands.

"Must be." Eden's gaze wandered to the window. She sighed.

Don't start thinking about Jerry. Don't look at Davis as a substitute. He's leaving, remember? Let it go. You'll find love…someday…when your time in the CIA is over.

When Mick and Tara returned, they were all smiles. Telltale traces of Tara's lipstick on his face gave away the outcome of their rendezvous. They finished the cinnamon buns, refilled their cups with the warm wine, and turned a football game on the television.

"I'd take you to do more sightseeing, but everything is closed today," Eden said, moving their drinks to the coffee table.

"That's okay. Georgia Tech, my favorite team, is playing. This should be good."

"I love football." She sank down on the sofa next to him.

A look of wonder spread across his face. "You do?"

"Yep, but I don't have a favorite college team. I'll root for yours."

The four friends settled into a pleasant afternoon of exciting football maneuvers, plentiful snacks, and a respite from challenging conversation. Eden spied Tara sneaking looks at her and Tom from time to time. *She'd love for us to hook up...be a foursome.* Eden smiled to herself. *It would be such fun...so normal. For a change.* She took a deep breath.

When Georgia Tech won the game, Mick and Tom jumped up out of their seats and danced around. Then, each grabbed his woman and kissed her. Mick and Tara stopped to stare at the kiss Tom gave Eden, as it was much more than a victory peck.

He grasped her to him in a tight hold while he deepened it. Eden's hands rested on his shoulders as his mouth ravaged hers. A soft moan escaped her throat. She was breathless when he finally let her go.

"What?" the major asked, facing his friends.

Mick raised his eyebrows, and Tara followed suit as they stared at him.

Tom blushed to the roots of his hair. "We won. A victory...uh...kiss is all." He lowered his gaze and returned to his seat.

"Here's hoping they win every game," Eden chimed in, raising her cup.

* * * *

The next morning, Tom awoke early and dressed in his service "A" uniform, the required attire for formal reporting. It didn't take him long to don the immaculately pressed outfit—green waist length dress coat, green trousers with khaki web belt, khaki long-sleeve button-up shirt, khaki tie, tie clasp, and black shoes. This was the uniform he only wore when having to report to headquarters. All the seams had creases that were sharp as knives.

Checking himself in the mirror, making sure his ribbons and badges were aligned properly, shaking off the memories of why he had earned them and the buddies he had lost, he was ready.

"Wow, I didn't think you could look better than you have, but this is amazing," Eden said, sipping coffee.

"Have to wear this when I'm reporting."

"I see. You can wear it for me anytime." She tightened the sash on her robe.

Tom turned his gaze from the mirror to Eden, who was dressed only in a light blue terry robe, the color of her eyes.

"And you can dress like that for me anytime, too." He chuckled.

She approached him. "Get serious for a minute. What do you expect to happen today?"

"I don't know. Never know quite what to expect."

"Okay. I'll rephrase. What do you want to happen?"

"Can't say. Brings bad luck."

Her face registered shock. "You're not superstitious?"

"Not exactly. Besides, wishing for something doesn't make it so. Hard work, being smart, loyal, and getting it done make it happen."

"What do you want?" She moved close enough to rest her palms on his chest.

"With you?" He closed his fingers around her waist.

"With the Marines. Well, maybe both."

"Not admitting anything here, but it might be nice if you and the service lined up at the same time."

She chuckled. "Then, I'll wish that for you."

"You'll be here when I get back, beautiful?" he whispered in her ear.

"With bells on."

"And nothing else?"

She giggled. "You'll have to return to find out."

Tom glanced at his watch. "Time to go if I'm going to make the eight o'clock train."

"Safe journey." Eden rose on her tiptoes to kiss him.

"See you tonight."

"I'll be waiting."

He walked outside and hailed a cab. New York City folk had not all returned from the holiday and traffic was light. The taxi whisked Tom down to Penn Station in no time. He bought his ticket for the Metroliner and grabbed a cup of coffee and a breakfast sandwich. When the gate opened, he was one of the first to board.

He took a window seat and chowed down, suddenly hungry. The train exited New York smoothly, picking up speed as it wended its way through New Jersey. When he finished eating, Tom sat back and stared out the window. The scenery flew by, but still he could make out houses and big buildings. As it passed into lower New Jersey, Tom gazed out onto a greener setting. He spied small houses with picket fences and his thoughts turned to Eden.

Too soon to be thinking about her that way. Hell, haven't even slept with her yet. What if she's terrible in bed? Lays there like a dead fish? He chuckled at the thought. *Not likely.* Something stirred inside him. The quest for adventure that had driven him to the Marines began to fade, replaced by the growing desire for a home life. He wondered what was going to happen today. Would it destroy his ability to settle down, if he wanted to?

The train arrived at Union Station before Tom had decided anything about his life. He shrugged and resolved to take what came from this meeting in stride. Afterward, there'd be plenty of time to figure out how to carve out a love life around his responsibilities as a Marine. He climbed into a taxi and headed for the Pentagon.

"Major Tom Davis reporting to Colonel Denny as ordered."

The lady behind the desk, a sergeant, smiled and picked up the phone. After hanging up, she said, "Go on in, major."

Tom took a deep breath, turned the knob and entered.

The room was well lit. In it, he saw Colonel Harlan Daniels, Commandant Mark Allen, Major General Patrick LaMotte, and two others sitting behind a long, mahogany table. Walking up to them, snapping to attention and saluting, he stated, "Major Tom Davis, reporting as ordered."

"At ease, major," General Allen said.

Tom dropped his salute and switched to the parade rest position—legs two feet apart, standing straight, hands at the small of his back.

"Major, we are here to talk about your performance and evaluation, along with your record," General LaMotte started.

A bead of sweat started to form on Tom's brow.

"Your performance in the Peterson incident was exemplary. It showed leadership skills that we need. To my left are Force Master Chief Link and Rear Admiral Patterson, SEAL command. Admiral Patterson?"

"Thank you, general. Major Davis, we at S.O.C.—Special Operations Command—were impressed with how you handled situations in Afghanistan and Germany. Your command and control caught our attention. We're offering you a command position with the Gunslingers. If you accept, you'll be cross trained with the SEALS and promoted to Lieutenant Colonel."

Major Davis smiled. It was a prestigious offer, and the promotion he had been looking for. "When will this take effect, sir?"

"Because the training's intense, you'll get two weeks of leave, then it's back to Afghanistan to command your unit until your replacement arrives. Since you're from Georgia, we're offering you Battalion Command in Kings Bay."

"I take it you're accepting the offer, major?" the general asked.

"Yes, sir, I am."

"Congratulations, colonel. Enjoy your two weeks. You're going to need the rest!" Master Chief Link gave an ominous grin.

"Thank you, sir." Davis said. He did an about face and left the review board.

As soon as he was outside and alone, Tom opened his phone and dialed. "Jennifer?"

"Tom? Is that you?" Though younger by a year, his sister had become his confidant.

"Hey, sis, guess what? Headquarters promoted me to Lieutenant Colonel. I'll be in command of the Gunslingers. And eventually, stationed back in Georgia."

"That's great. When'll I see you?"

"Soon," Tom replied, and then hung up. Tom boarded the Metroliner, bound for New York City and Eden's apartment. He opened his cell again.

"Hey, major. Wasn't sure I'd hear from you. On a jet to a secret mission?" Eden couldn't hide the anxiety in her voice.

"Not yet, beautiful. On my way to New York. I told you I was coming back."

"People say that—oh wait, correction—*guys* say that all the time and don't mean it."

"Don't lump me in with guys like that. I meant it. I'll be back by six. How about dinner?"

"You're really coming back. Fantastic. Lucky for me."

"Pick you up at seven?"

"Works for me."

"Dress to kill. I'm feeling great, and we're gonna celebrate."

"Good news?"

"You'll see."

"How long you staying?"

"I'll tell you tonight."

"Teasing me, hmm? I'll find a way to tease you back."

He laughed. "I love challenges."

"Good. 'Cause I like to challenge. I've got just the dress, too."

"Can't wait to see you in it…and out of it." He snickered.

"Planning to make a pass, major?"

"Never planning, only hoping."

"Good. I hate over-confident men."

"I love confident women. See you tonight."

"Wait. Don't hang up. Should we invite Mick and Tara to tag along?"

"Good idea. Need to include them on this one."

"Got the perfect place nearby. Stupid as this may sound—I miss you already. How'd you get under my skin so fast?"

"Personality?" he asked.

"Nah. Broad shoulders, maybe." She chuckled.

"See you tonight."

* * * *

A little thrill shot up her spine. Being with Tom was exciting. She was beginning to trust him. And he was attractive as hell. A little sadness crept into her heart. *How much time will we have together. A day? A week at most? Then, he's on his way, and I'm on mine. Will I see him again…ever?* She chewed her lip as these negative thoughts circled through her mind.

Eden searched her closet for the right dress. Then, she spied it, hiding in the back. A little dark purple, silk one with a halter neck and a skirt that stopped mid-thigh. She pulled it out and tried it on. It had generous armholes that revealed a bit of her breasts. *No bra with this baby.*

A saucy smile curled her lips as she pictured the expression on the major's face when he saw her in the sexy number. *He's a goner, for sure.* She giggled. For the first time in a long time, she missed having a close, single friend. Her old high school girlfriends would approve. She heard her best friend Katie's voice in her head—*Make him chase you until you catch him.*

Tara was her best friend now, but she was married and hanging with Mick most of the time. They didn't giggle together about being single, men, sex, and all the torments and temptations surrounding finding a man. She sighed. Life had been so much about surviving, hiding, kill or be killed lately that she had missed the innocent sweetness of new love.

Eden laid the dress on the bed as she searched for the right shoes. Hiding in a back corner of the closet was a pair of silver sling-backs with four-inch heels. *Gotta practice walking in these.* She slipped them on then paced up and down the room a few times.

Hell, if I'm not going to see him again...I want him. Have from the first night. Tonight's the night. I can't hold out any longer. A very special celebration. She laughed to herself. *The major gets lucky.*

She ran water and poured in a little lilac bubble bath. Soaking in the tub, she thought about Tom, about that kiss after the game. *He's a passionate man.* In spite of the hot water, her whole body shivered as she let her mind drift to what it might be like, making love with Major Davis. *I feel like I'm sixteen years old, going on a first date. This is goofy.* But she couldn't stop smiling.

Escaping her troubled thoughts by losing herself in Tom's arms then spending the night safely locked in his embrace brought a smile of anticipation to her face and a lightness too new to her heart. Eden soaped up a washcloth and rubbed it over her arms and chest. The roughness made her skin tingle. She closed her eyes and imagined the major's stubbled chin replacing the cloth.

But her bubble burst when she realized he'd be clean shaven. *Regulations. But that's not all bad.* A smile settled on her face

when she envisioned resting her palm on his smooth cheek. *No beard burn from that kiss.*
Are we celebrating a new mission? Is he going in harm's way? She chewed her lip.

A chill ran through her body. She stood up and pulled the plug. As she wrapped a towel around her chest, she hardened her resolve. *No matter how dangerous, I'm not going to whine. I'm going to be strong. I'm no wimp, and the last thing he needs is a sniveling, complaining female.*

She dried off and threw on her sexiest panties—black satin with see-through on the sides. The dress was cool on her warm skin as she slid the fine fabric up her body and fastened it around her neck. Next was makeup. She chuckled to herself over how it took so much longer to make yourself look like you weren't wearing any than it took simply to apply the stuff. But tonight was special, she had to look her best.

Eden was used to grabbing rare nights with a man she cared for, not knowing when the opportunity would come again. Her life with Jerry had been one of stolen evenings, uncommon weekends spent together, hiding in each other's arms away from the enemy and from the world. She wondered what it would be like to grow tired of the presence of her man, to need to have a night away with the girls. She envied women who lived like that.

Eden figured she wasn't destined to marry someone safe, like a businessman or a doctor. Her family had been involved in the CIA for years, starting with her grandparents. Danger was a constant in the Wyatt family, passed down from generation to generation.

Her parents had died working for the agency. Shot down on a plane that had veered into Chinese territory when returning from a mission. The wreckage had never been recovered. She had been only ten at the time. Eden had gone to live with her grandparents. They were warm, loving people dedicated to the survival of democracy. They had become her role models. And so she had ended up at the Agency, like those before her.

Still, her heart yearned to live a normal life, to be relaxed instead of vigilant, bored instead of adjusting to a new environment, hiding out constantly. The desire for the traditional white picket fence, an image she had discarded as a teen, had crept into her dreams. The wish for daring missions had been replaced by the wish for children and learning to use a slow cooker. She attributed it to age and too many bad experiences, too much death.

Then, Major Davis had come along, sweeping her away, stealing her heart with his sweetness and his handsome presence, filling her with desire. *So much like Jerry. Smart, proud, strong.* She couldn't resist him, though she tried. Or that's what she told herself.

She applied the last touch—moist, pink lipstick—and looked in the mirror. *Not bad.* The doorbell rang. She glanced at her watch. It was only five thirty. She checked through the peephole then opened the door to admit Mick and Tara.

"Wow, Eden. You look fantastic." Tara said, entering the apartment first.

"You can say that again," her husband mumbled, his gaze moving up and down Eden's body.

"The major won't be expecting this," Tara added, unbuttoning her coat.

"It's a surprise attack," Eden said, closing the door and locking all three locks.

"You're armed and dangerous," Mick put in.

"Exactly what I had in mind. Care for a drink while we wait?"

Chapter Four

Washington, D.C.

Tom looked out the window as the Metroliner sped along at a breakneck speed, heading for New York. He shifted in his seat, turning his gaze to the other passengers then to a newspaper in his lap. He couldn't sit still or focus on any one thing for long. He was beyond jumpy.

This promotion was a big accomplishment and, coupled with the new woman taking over his heart, Tom was ready to burst. He couldn't stop smiling and was itching to tell everyone on board how lucky he was, how happy he was, how perfect his life was turning out to be.

Sure, he still didn't have all the facts about Eden, but he was confident in his instincts about her being on the right side, as well as interested in him. He didn't know how interested, but he hoped to find out tonight, while they still had a couple of weeks together. He knew by her response to his kisses that she was a passionate woman, but exactly how hot remained to be seen. He looked forward to finding out.

It's not like he hadn't had his fair share of women. Some never saw beyond his rank, anxious as they were to snag a man with a decent income and a future. He was onto the wiles of those, having fallen for one or two and learned the hard way. No longer taken in by an easy or a two-faced woman, Tom had guarded his heart, waiting for the right one to come along.

Maybe Eden was the one. She was different. She wouldn't see dollar signs when she heard about his promotion. She'd see Tom Davis, the man, before the lieutenant colonel. Direct, smart, honest—he hoped—and gorgeous, she was his kind of woman. Now, he was heading home to her and could hardly wait.

Can't this train move any faster? He went to the club car, the bathroom, and back again, but there was still an hour and a half to go. When the engine finally pulled into Penn Station, Tom was the first one off. He snagged a taxi and sat back, beaming, as he rode up the avenue to reconnect with the beauty he hoped soon to call his own.

After she buzzed, he took the stairs two at a time. He heard the click of the first of her locks as he neared her door. Anticipation turned to excitement in his blood.

Tom's heart skipped a beat when he saw Eden. His jaw dropped and "Wow" was all he could say. The corner of Eden's lips curled up at his reaction, forming a small, but self-satisfied grin. Davis scooped her into his arms and kissed her passionately. She pulled back, whispering in his ear, "later." He got the message, exchanging a knowing smile with her. *Does that mean I'm getting lucky tonight with her? Damn. I hope so.*

The two couples left the building, walking east until they reached Mythology, the Greek restaurant Eden had chosen. They were seated at a quiet table in the corner.

"Eden said you were in D.C. today, at Headquarters. What's up?" Mick questioned.

Tom grinned at his friends and put down his beer. "I was offered a promotion and new assignment today."

Everybody spoke at once.

"Really?"

"Congratulations."

"Wow."

After the excitement died down, Mick asked, "What happened?"

"They were impressed after our mission to recue your sorry ass," he answered, grinning at Mick.

"Who's an ass?" Mick asked.

They laughed.

Eden smacked Tom's shoulder. "And?"

"They offered me a new command and a promotion, effective immediately. I am now a Lieutenant Colonel and start training to take command of the Gunslingers."

"That's awesome" came from Mick.

"Congratulations," said Tara.

Eden kissed him.

When they broke apart, Tara asked, "What's Gunslinger?"

"It's a special operations unit. The elite. I'll cross-train with the SEALS before taking command."

Eden leaned in and kissed him again, whispering in his ear, "Tell me more later."

Tom saw Mick and Tara glance at each other and grin. About this time, the waiter brought their food. Eden settled back into her chair and picked up her fork.

"Looks great. Good choice, Eden." Tom said, looking over his plate.

"What? The restaurant or you?"

"Both," Tom answered, cutting his lamb. She grinned at him.

For desert, they all had Baklava and Turkish coffee. Tom picked up the check, though Mick gave him a hard time.

"We're celebrating my promotion. It's my treat." His buddy couldn't argue.

They walked home together, separating and bidding goodnight on the stairs. It took Eden a minute or two to undo all the locks on her door. The matchstick was in place. She let out a breath and swung the door wide.

After they hung up their jackets, she turned to him. "How will your promotion change your life? Will you be shopping for a wife? If you are, don't look in my aisle."

"Wife? Oh, no, not ready for that one yet."

Not just any woman will do. If she's on the shelf waiting for me to pluck her off, she'll have a long wait. But maybe a woman like you—gorgeous, smart, and fearless—could change my mind.

"Hey, Mr. Dangerously Sexy, up for a nightcap?" She licked her bottom lip and rested her hand on her hip.

"Sure. Can you do a martini? Shaken, not stirred?"

"Of course." She crossed the room to the bar and pulled out the ingredients. Tom watched her, taking in every seductive sway of her body. The fabric clung to her curves, capturing his attention, sizzling all the way to his groin. *What would happen if she danced in that dress? I'd probably come right here.*

"Olive or onion?" she asked.

"Olive. What about you?" He couldn't keep his gaze off her. It lingered on her breasts before sliding down, taking in every hot, sinful inch of her. Desire rocketed through his veins. He had to have her.

"I'm a vodka tonic woman," she answered.

He smiled. "Ah, like on New Year's. I remember." He wandered over when she had her back to him.

His hand on her bare shoulder startled her. "Oh, I didn't see you. A stealth move. Well done."

From behind, he snaked his arm around her waist. Her perfume called to him, enticing him to kiss her, touch her. When she leaned back against him and closed her eyes, he pushed her hair aside to reach her neck.

"Did you wear this dress just for me?" he whispered. His hands itched to slid up the front of her and cup her breasts. The halter neckline prevented him from viewing her cleavage, frustrating him. He wanted her, wanted her bad.

"How'd you guess?"

"Great choice," he said, nuzzling her neck, causing him to begin to harden. With one hand, he could rip that halter off. The dress would fall, and she'd be his. His to look at. His to touch. The idea made more blood rush between his legs.

Get a grip. I'm a Marine, not a schoolboy with a crush. Control yourself. But lust ruled, setting him on fire. He could have pushed her away, but chose to give in to his burning need. *She didn't wear this to turn me down. I've got to try and hope for the best.*

* * * *

Eden gasped as he turned her and pulled her to him, pressing her chest against his, taking her mouth with a demanding kiss. Heat pooled in her body as she softened in his embrace. When he let her go, she was breathless.

"Whoa, you're passionate, aren't you?" She looked up into his eyes. "Guess it's my lucky day." Eden skimmed her arms around his waist. She peered up at him from under perfectly blackened lashes, her lips slightly swollen from his previous assault.

"Try that again, L.C.," she whispered.

He cocked an eyebrow at her. "Is that an order?"

"Uh huh. A direct order." She pressed her hips against him.

He leaned over and captured her mouth again. Slowly, he swiped his tongue against her lips, and she opened for him to deepen the kiss.

Dangerous Love Lost & Found

Before she lost control, Eden stepped back, picked up her glass, and sauntered over to the sofa. Tom joined her there.

They finished their drinks in silence. Eden sensed the electricity. The sparks between them were almost palpable.

Tom plaited his fingers through her golden locks. "Beautiful," he muttered.

When she turned toward him, he placed his hand on her waist, pulling her to him for another kiss. A soft moan from her throat gave her away. *Betrayed by my own body.* Tom picked up on her lack of resistance and tightened his grip. When he let go, Eden could barely catch her breath.

"When do the maneuvers begin?" Her gaze searched his.

"I was being respectful." His eyes were clear blue with no hint of guile or deceit.

"By not moving in? Making a pass?"

A quirky smile lifted his lips. "Right."

"Aren't you the sweetest?" She palmed his cheek.

"I've wanted to make a pass at you from the moment I saw you hiding behind Mick's front door," he whispered in her ear.

"You've got a lot of self-control…that was days ago."

"I always respect a lady."

Eden's fingers closed over his shoulders. "Guess I didn't need to be on guard with you."

"Never."

She moved her hand slowly down his chest. "Safe then, eh?"

"Completely. And now?" He raised his eyebrows in question.

"Maybe it's time to take our celebration to another level. Hell, I'm not easy for a lowly major, but a lieutenant colonel…that's something else."

He laughed.

She peered up at him as he grazed her lips. His hands on her waist pulled her closer. When she opened, he caressed her tongue with his. A shudder ran up her spine as he slid his fingers up her ribcage and closed them over her breast. Her breathing was ragged as heat again traveled to her core. She wanted more. *I've resisted long enough. I want him. Who knows how much time we'll have?*

Tom eased her down on the sofa, continuing to massage her gently as his lips traveled to her neck. She unbuttoned his shirt and slipped her hand inside, only to find an undershirt.

"Damn. Do you always wear an undershirt?"

"Regulations."

"Tell your superiors it takes the spontaneity out of lovemaking, will you?"

"I doubt that was taken into consideration when they made the reg."

She ripped the shirt up and out of his belt. Then, she slipped her hand under the soft cotton T-shirt and up his abs to his pecs. He groaned when her fingers made contact with his skin.

"Oh, God, that sexy, hairy chest. Wanted to touch you since you came out of the shower wearing a towel." She continued to explore his pecs. "I think I'm in heaven," she mumbled.

The vibration of his laugh made her nipples harden. He reached up and deftly undid the hooks at the neck of her halter-top. He peeled it down like she was a banana and he was starving.

He stopped when it reached her waist. His eyes feasted on her breasts, more than a handful, bared for his view. "Wow, gorgeous. Amazing." He continued to stare as his fingers closed around her flesh. Then, he bent his head and kissed it.

She ran her fingers through the short stubble of his hair and kissed the top of his head. "You like?"

"Are you kidding? I love," he said, devouring her right breast before moving to the left.

Eden arched her back to give him easier access. His lips and tongue glided over the skin, paying particular attention to each peak, driving her wild. She resumed unbuttoning his shirt and shoved the undershirt up with difficulty. Now, most of his torso was bare. Pushing up, she made chest-to-chest contact. She took in a sharp breath at the feeling, a prelude to a total skin-to-skin sensation when making love.

Color crept up Tom's chest and neck, giving away his arousal. Her legs were trapped between his, making the sloughing off of her dress impossible. She wanted him, badly, and the ache was growing. Her hand reached for his belt buckle. That stopped him. He looked up.

Desire flamed in his blue eyes, making the shade deeper. She stared at him, not caring if he saw her naked lust. The fire was taking over, and only he could put it out.

Dangerous Love Lost & Found

Eden leaned forward and pushed his shirt off his shoulders. He slipped his arms out of the shirt then ripped the undershirt over his head and off. She sighed as her eyes drank in his masculine beauty. His chest was wide and well-muscled. Covered with light hair and sporting six-pack abs, he looked fit and sexy as hell. Simply the sight of him stoked her passion.

Tom pushed up to his knees. He sat back, placing one hand on each side of her skimpy dress, and began to slide it down.

"No objections?" He cocked his head a bit.

"Only to the slow speed of this maneuver. Kick it into high gear, Davis."

He chuckled before returning to the task at hand. When the garment reached her ankles, he folded it neatly and placed it on the coffee table.

"So military," she murmured, smiling.

Finally, she watched him admire the black satin bikinis. Tom ran his palms from her shoulders to her knees, then curled his fingers around her slim, shapely thighs, rubbing his thumbs on the inside long enough to elicit a gasp from her. Eden gave a little squeak, making him grin. His gaze raked her body as her hands, shaking slightly, unbuckled his belt and unzipped his fly. He leaned down to kiss her belly and run his hand down over her core.

She pushed his pants down. He hooked a finger in each side of her waistband and slowly slid the panties down her legs.

"I feel like there should be some stripper music playing," she whispered.

He stopped. "I can go find some if you—"

"Don't you dare get up."

He burst into laughter. "I have you right where I want you."

"Yeah, you do," she said softly, reaching for his neck.

He leaned down, and she took his mouth. His fingers combed through her hair as she moaned into him.

Tom pulled back. "Now who's slowing us down?" He quickly slid the panties down to her knees, where she pulled her legs through and tossed them on a chair. His gaze heated her skin as it traveled up and down her body, stopping to drink in key sights. "You're incredibly beautiful. Your body is perfect." He bent to kiss her belly.

Wantonness mixed with shyness in her blood. Tom was new, but so hot, she couldn't stop herself. Eden pushed to a sitting position. "Come on." She took his hand.

He got up, removed his pants, and folded them neatly, placing them on the chair next to his shirt.

"You're such a Marine." She laughed.

"Is that bad?"

"Better a neat man than a sloppy one."

When he was done, he held out his hand. She laced her fingers with his and led him into the bedroom. Tom pulled the covers down and let her get in first. After removing his boxers, he followed her quickly, scooping her into his embrace, holding her body up against his. She could feel all of him next to her. His arousal was unmistakable.

His hands skimmed over her back and bottom. He stopped to squeeze her small rear then pulled her closer. She raised her knee and hooked her leg around his waist. Tom ran his hand down the back of her thigh then slid it inside and up. When his fingers came in contact with her core, she flinched.

"Too much?" He raised his head and made eye contact. "Did I hurt you?"

She put a hand on each side of his face and pulled him to her for a passionate kiss. "A little shy…don't know you as well as I'd like."

"We can stop. Have tea and chat until you know me well enough."

She smacked his shoulder gently. "And what would you do if I said 'okay'?"

"Probably panic." He chuckled.

"Let's try again," she whispered in his ear. He touched her, but this time got only a soft moan as response. He stroked her gently, but insistently. Her hips began to move with him.

"Oh my God, Tom…"

"Hey. You called me Tom. Didn't think you knew my first name."

She chuckled. "Saving it for a passionate moment." She reached down and curled her fingers around him. He responded immediately. His mouth came down on hers, hard and demanding. Her other arm snaked around his middle. She hugged him to her, arching into him. He tore his lips from hers and kissed the length of her neck then farther down.

When he reached her breasts, he slipped one finger then another inside her. Her rear rose right off the bed when his lips pulled gently on her hard nub.

"Tom, do it, do it. Take me. Oh God, what are you waiting for?"

"Ladies first." He continued to pump his fingers in and out of her and tease her peak.

With his words, her muscles tensed, her hips bucked, and her arms tightened around his chest. The fire growing inside her burst wide open, shooting sparks to every part of her body. Burying her face in his neck, eyes closed, she groaned. Panting, she raised her head to peer into his eyes. "That was…that was…" She stopped, at a loss for words.

"You're amazing. You went off like a rocket."

"That's it—explosive, skyrockets…firecrackers."

Tom grabbed the condom he'd deposited on the nightstand. He grinned before he parted her legs, sliding his hands down to her ankles then back to her thighs again. "Nice." Then, he shifted them under her knees, lifting them off the bed and onto his shoulders. "Let's do this right," he muttered.

"Aye, aye, Colonel." Her relaxed limbs were putty in his hands. He tore the packet open with his teeth and covered himself. Once he had her the way he wanted, he rubbed himself against her warm flesh and slid in easily.

"Holy Hell," he moaned.

Looking up, she saw him close his eyes for a bit as sweat coated his forehead. He pushed up farther making her gasp.

"You okay?" he asked.

She nodded. "A good fit," she murmured.

"Hell yeah."

He began to move in and out of her slowly. Eden licked the salty flavor of Tom off his shoulder. "Oh, that feels so…amazing." She rocked her hips with his. They synchronized perfectly, achieving a rhythm that slowly increased in speed. Her fingers dug into his shoulders, feeling the power of his muscles. As she arched into him again, Tom pushed up on his arms, peering down.

When her stare made contact with his, she saw a look of love mixed with raw desire. His eyes glowed, a slight blush colored his cheeks, and he looked more handsome than ever. Eden's heart lurched at his expression of unmasked, naked adoration. A small smile curled her lips as her hand touched his cheek ever so gently.

The rhythm increased and passion began to flow in her veins once more. The tension spiraled up slowly, growing as he moved faster. "Tom." She dug her fingertips into his arms.

"Baby, baby, baby," he said, sweat beading up on his shoulders.

He reached down to touch her, sending her control south. Her hips moved automatically as she croaked out his name again. One chuckle slipped from his mouth before release ripped through him. He moaned "Beautiful Eden" as he thrust hard once more then stopped.

The heavy breathing was almost audible in the quiet room. The lovers clung to each other as heart rates returned to normal. Tom leaned down and tenderly kissed her forehead. Eden ran her thumb along the top of his shoulder then pulled her chin up, awaiting a kiss. He grazed her lips with his before he pulled out of her and rolled onto his side.

"Be right back," he said, sliding out of bed and trotting to the bathroom. Eden stretched on the mattress and sported her widest grin in two years.

Tom stopped and looked down. "Now, this is a great view."

"Oh? As good as the Grand Canyon?"

"Better."

"Flattery will get you everywhere," she said, tugging on his hand.

"As long as everywhere includes you," he quipped, lying down next to her.

Eden curled into him, resting her head on his chest. He slung his arm around her, easing her in tight against him before he pulled up the covers.

"This is the best," she murmured.

"You're the best."

"Do they give out medals for lovemaking? Can I nominate you for a gold star?"

He laughed. "I don't think so."

"Guess, it'll have to be my own gold star then."

He kissed her hair. "It's a two-way street, Eden. You were incredible. Turned me on like never before."

She pushed up on her elbows. "Yeah?"

"Hell yeah. You're fire on legs."

"So are you. Love your body." *Love all of you, but not saying that now.*

"Two weeks with you…like winning the lottery," he said, placing a kiss on the tip of her nose.

Eden snuggled down into his embrace and closed her eyes. "Goodnight, my handsome Lieutenant Colonel."

"I knew the *Tom* thing was too good to last." He sighed.

"Sweet dreams, Tom," she whispered.

"Thank you. Goodnight, beautiful."

He rolled onto his side, tucking Eden into his body, folding his arm around her. She felt safe, listening to the beat of his heart and enveloped in his warmth. She smiled, closed her eyes, and sleep came quickly.

Several hours later, before dawn peeped through the cracks in her curtains, Eden turned over. Her hand came in contact with someone. She became partially conscious.

"Jerry?" she whispered, her hand running up and down the figure's back.

"It's me," he said softly.

Suddenly, her eyes flew open, and she groped for the gun she had hidden in the sheets. "Who the hell?"

The man reached over and fastened his large hand around her wrist, stopping her cold. "It's me—Tom. Eden…Tom Davis," he repeated. "I'm the guy who just made love to you?"

She rubbed her eyes with her free hand and peered at him in the darkness. "Tom?"

"Yeah. You're okay. Safe." Yet, he still held her wrist clamped to the bed.

Eden blew out a breath. "Oh, God. I thought…never mind. Sorry about that." She stroked his cheek.

"No worries. Not gonna go for your gun now, are you?"

She kissed him. "Nope."

Tom released her and pulled her closer to him. "Come over here. How'd you get so far away? And who's Jerry?"

"Sometimes, I get restless during the night. Jerry was the only man I ever loved." She spoke the second part softly.

"Was?"

"He's gone now. Killed. Murdered."

"I'm so sorry." Tom drew her against his chest and kissed her hair.

"Thanks. I don't want to talk about Jerry."

"I understand."

The sensation of his hard chest touching her soft one turned her on. Teased by his chest hair, her nipples hardened. He closed his fingers around her breast. She lifted her leg and hooked it around his waist. He moaned and changed his position so that his erection settled between her thighs.

"With a little shift in position, I could be inside you in a heartbeat," he whispered.

"Is that a threat or a promise?"

Tom reached his long arm up to the nightstand and retrieved another condom. He leaned back to cover himself. "Now, where were we?"

The lovers tried to resume their former position, but only ended up tangled together. They laughed as they moved one leg here and another one there.

Eden wrapped her fingers around him. "Wow. You're like a rock."

"Being here with you, naked, does that to me."

"That's wonderful." She emitted a soft sound like the purr of a cat and again twined her leg around his waist.

"Think we've got it this time." Tom thrust forward slowly.

Eden sighed as he entered her. "Oh, yeah."

He chuckled as he began to move his hips. Eden was trapped in a position where she couldn't move, so she simply lay back and let Tom run the show. He pumped into her, sending fire through her veins. Sexual tension coiled tighter within her with each thrust. He buried his face in her neck and licked her.

"Oh, God. Tom." She shuddered as the intensity grew to a breaking point. He cupped her bottom, pulled it tighter to him, and held it there as he increased the speed and drove into her harder and harder. Eden gripped his shoulders with a death-like grasp, digging her fingers into his muscles as her insides contracted around him and warmth coursed through her veins.

"Damn. Eden." He groaned loudly as he plunged once more and stopped. Two sweaty, slippery bodies heaved as the lovers tried to catch their breath. Tom kissed her shoulder, and she slid her nails gently down his back.

Finally, their breathing returned to normal. Tom made a dash to the bathroom and returned quickly. He lowered himself next to her.

"Never knew a nightmare could have such a happy ending." Eden cracked up, laughing until she cried.

Tom bundled her into his embrace. "You're amazing, woman."

She allowed herself to gaze at him lovingly because the darkness partially hid her expression. She cupped his cheek. "Don't need any sleep meds when you're here." She stretched and yawned.

He chuckled. "You saying I put you to sleep?"

"Saying you relax me to the point where it's a chore to stay awake."

"Much better."

Eden kissed him. "Goodnight, honey." Then, she closed her eyes.

"Hmm. From Davis to Tom. From Tom to honey. I'm making progress."

Then, the only sound in the room was even breathing.

Chapter Five

Eden and Tom were jarred awake by the telephone. Eden's cell was next to the bed and the ring, which was the opening from Edvard Grieg's "Morning," woke them up. She checked to see who was calling then slipped on Tom's discarded T-shirt and scampered into the living room, shutting the door behind her.

"Yes, Sumner. I'm here."

"Sleeping in?" he joked.

"I'm on leave, right?"

"Of course."

"So, yes, at seven o'clock, I'm sleeping in." She chuckled.

"I got approval to give you two more weeks until your next assignment. Enjoy yourself. Then, I'm handing you back to Lynn. She'll brief you."

"Here or overseas?"

"Don't know and couldn't say. This isn't a secure line."

"Oh, right. Sorry. So, Lynn's moving up from secretary to assistant now?"

"Still secretary, but the most efficient kind. She likes you, specifically asked to work with you on this one."

"Good. I like Lynn. She doesn't waste time."

"That's my Eden. To the point and getting things done."

Tom opened the living room door and sneezed. There was a brief silence on the other end of the phone.

"Oh. I see. Perhaps you're not *my* Eden anymore. Maybe you belong to someone else?"

"Probing will get you nowhere, Mr. Smith."

"Now, it's Mr. Smith. Getting formal, aren't you? Have fun with your new playmate and be ready to go back to work in two weeks. Lynn'll be in touch. Stay safe, will ya? If you need anything, I'm here."

"Thanks, Sumner."

Tom sat down next to her on the sofa. He'd put on boxers but nothing else. Her eyes feasted on his fabulous chest and shoulders.

"Sorry. Did I interrupt a private conversation?"

"Just my boss."

"You're not working today?"

"I got the okay to take two weeks off."

"To be with me?"

She nodded.

"That's awesome." He clasped her in a bear hug.

"Gotta breathe...," she gasped.

"Oh. Sorry. Sometimes I don't know my own strength."

"But I do." She snickered. "How about food?"

"I'm starved. Put me to work." He pushed to his feet.

"Order around a Lieutenant Colonel? How could I?"

"Easy. I'm your slave. Awaiting orders, ma'am."

Together, they cooked up bacon and eggs. Tom set the table, made the toast, and turned the bacon while Eden was busy with the eggs. She tried to ignore how easily they worked together. She was so comfortable with him that it seemed as if she had known him all her life.

His playful pat on her bottom or cupping of her breast as he passed by kept a low level of arousal constant in her body. His physical affection warmed her heart. Even Jerry hadn't done that...well, not in a long time.

At breakfast, she opened the newspaper to the entertainment section.

"Do you like classical music?" she asked, scooping some scrambled eggs onto her fork.

"I do."

"Peer Gynt is playing at the Philharmonic tonight. Maybe we can get tickets."

"Great. Can you do it online?"

Eden powered up her laptop. When Tom had polished off his breakfast, he went online and bought two tickets.

After breakfast, making the bed turned into a pillow fight, which ended in another lovemaking session. Eden wanted to spend the day in bed with Tom, but put aside her desires to show him around town. She rattled off a list of things they could do outside the bedroom, and Tom picked a visit to the American Museum of Natural History. They spent two hours checking out the dinosaurs and taxidermied animals. He bought her lunch in a romantic bistro on Columbus Avenue.

The light from the fireplace in the small restaurant cast shadows on Tom, emphasizing the planes created by his cheekbones. Her gaze was riveted to his handsome face, and the loving expression she saw there. They shared a bread pudding dessert, feeding each other like lovers.

When she took a gander in the ladies' room mirror, the healthy glow of a well-loved woman reflected back at her, and she put her powder blush back in her bag. She hadn't looked so good in a long time. She hadn't remembered how much being adored showed. The once sad, frightened woman suddenly couldn't stop smiling, and she had her lieutenant colonel to thank.

Coffee had arrived when she returned to the table. Eden laughed with Tom as he regaled her with funny stories from his childhood.

"I wish you could tell me about Afghanistan," she said, sipping coffee.

"Maybe someday." He took her hand, curling his large fingers over her small palm. "But it isn't nearly as funny as the day Mick and I brought our big toad, Jericho, to Mrs. Fundy's class for show and tell."

She grinned. "I'm sure. I bet I'd be impressed if I saw you in action."

"You already have, several times." He chuckled.

She swiped at his shoulder, but grinned, too. "You know what I mean."

"I'd rather you never see that. Never be near me when there's danger." He cupped both hands around hers. "I want you safe. Always."

"Wish I could promise that."

"Let's not talk about it." He raised her hand to his lips.

"Okay. Which dinosaur did you like the best?"

Their sightseeing ended with a walk home, arms around each other to brace against the winterish wind. Bright sunshine reflected her mood. Eden rustled up some hash and eggs for a quick bite before the concert. Neither one was very hungry after their big lunch…for food, anyway.

The evening was chilly. Eden donned a black, cashmere sweater and black, silk pants. She slipped on black, leather ankle boots. Tom dressed in the living room. When she opened the bedroom door, she gulped. *I'll never get tired of seeing him in uniform.* She coughed to cover up her response.

"Wow. You look amazing," he said.

"All in black. Like a black cat." She twirled in front of him.

"And just as soft…"

"Don't forget the claws."

He laughed. "How could I?"

Tom held her coat then took her hand as they descended the stairs. He hailed a cab, and they rode in silence to Lincoln Center. The soft lights of the impressive structure, consisting of several buildings, with lots of glass and stunning sculptures, surrounding a fountain, gave her goose bumps. Tom stopped to stare at the beautiful architecture and to snap a picture with his phone.

"No matter how many times I've been here, I still get excited." She hung on his arm.

"It's amazing. Never seen anything like it."

"And the music will be the best." Eden laced her fingers with his.

Once they were settled into their seats, he looked around at the elegant auditorium. Every seat was filled. The conductor appeared to a hearty round of applause. Tom took Eden's hand and rested it on his thigh. She sighed and sat back, but her eyes darted about, checking for anything out of the ordinary. *So many people. Easy to hide here. Sneak in a gun.*

When she didn't spot any suspicious people, Eden forced thoughts about danger out of her mind and let the soothing melody wash over her. A sense of contentment flowed through her, due in part to the music, but mainly to the company of Tom Davis.

After Jerry, she had vowed never to love again. *Too dangerous.* After a year or two, it had become ingrained. She had locked her heart away. Other men had tried to worm their way into her affections. But her guard was strong. When Tom had appeared, she didn't think twice about it. He was simply an attractive guy who needed a place to stay.

Then, he had executed a successful sneak attack on her heart, and she was surprised. Did she need him? *Eden Wyatt doesn't need anyone.* Did she want him? *Hell, yeah.*

Eden closed her eyes for a moment, afraid of the images that might reappear. But she breathed a sigh when all she saw was a sexy vision of Tom, and then the two of them romping around a green field in the middle of nowhere. *Must be the song.*

Tom tugged on her hand. "You okay?"

She nodded and shot him a big smile. He patted her before turning his attention back to the performance. *Now, if I could kill Mushin Musa Ali's brothers...I could have a life. Maybe a life with Tom?* She shook her head. *Who'd want to settle in with a killer? A wanted woman? No man in his right mind. Two weeks of heaven. Then, I'll let him go.*

A moment of sadness brought a deep sigh and frown. Tom squeezed her fingers. She turned her gaze to his. She read concern in his eyes, so she kissed the tip of her finger and placed it on his lips. Though he gave a small nod, the worried look didn't leave his face.

After the intermission, she cuddled closer to him, though it wasn't easy in the small, hard-backed seats. Eden scrunched down and rested her head on his shoulder. He took her hand again, and they listened to the rest of the concert in silence. From time to time, Tom rubbed his thumb over the back of her hand. His gentle touch kept the simmer of arousal active in her veins.

When the concert finished, the Philharmonic got a standing ovation. Tom held her coat for her then she hugged his arm as they headed into the icy night.

"Never get a cab now...too many people looking."

"Let's try anyway."

A taxi stopped in front of a man and woman. The man glanced over at Tom and stepped back. "You first, soldier."

"Thank you. My girl is freezing."

My girl? Eden smiled. *I like it.*

Tom opened the door for her. The cab headed uptown.

"Thank you for the concert. I loved it."

"Me, too. And your dinner was just the right thing."

"I'm not much of a cook. Haven't had time. I travel a lot." *Shit! Shut up, Eden.*

Tom looked hard at her. "Travel agent keeps you hopping, eh?"

She smiled quickly then looked away. *Never had such a hard time lying before.*

The apartment was chilly when they entered. A window was cracked open. Eden went right into high alert. She pulled a gun from the coat closet and held it up as she approached the open window.

Holding aim on the fire escape, she called to Tom, "Please close it." She kept him covered while he shut it and turned the lock. "That wasn't open when we left."

"I opened it after I showered. To let out the steam."

"Oh. Okay. Didn't notice." She replaced the gun and took a deep breath.

"You're safe with me, Eden. Trust me."

Tom, there's so much you don't know.

She hung up her coat and kept silent. He came up behind her and put his hands on her upper arms. Eden jumped.

"Hey, hey. It's okay, beautiful."

Leaning back against him, the firmness of his body gave her comfort.

"What is this you're wearing?" He rubbed the fabric of her sweater between his thumb and forefinger.

"Cashmere."

"Wow. Let's see..." He moved his hands around and closed his fingers over her breasts. "Oh, my God. Softest thing next to your skin." He buried his face in her neck, placing small kisses up and down the sensitive column.

She shivered. The dormant fire inside her jumped to life. She pressed her hips back against his.

"If you're gonna do that..." He turned her around and drew her into his embrace for a heat-seeking kiss.

Passion took over, driving her fears from her mind. Her senses ruled. She took his face in both her hands and returned the warmth of his kiss before inching closer to the bedroom.

"Eden, honey," he moaned, his hands wandering over her body.

His touch fueled her fire. Gentle, but insistent, exploring and coaxing, his fingers raised a need in her that begged to be fulfilled.

"Come on. We're wasting time." She took his hand, led him into the bedroom, and closed the door.

* * * *

A loud bang jolted Tom and Eden awake. Instantly alert, Eden spun around, grabbed a gun from under the mattress, and aimed at the door.

"There's one on your side, too," she whispered.

Tom grabbed the pistol at the same time that the door burst open. A shadow fell in the doorway. Eden double tapped it—one shot to the chest and the second perfectly in his head. Tom double tapped a second silhouette coming in fast behind the first.

They jumped out of bed and pressed their backs against the wall on each side of the doorway. Eden held her breath.

Tom whispered to her, "I'm going to check for more. Stay here for a sec."

Quickly ducking his head around the corner to look, he saw two more men in the next room. One fired, missing, as Tom pulled back in time. Eden raised her gun, her eyes wide.

"There are two more in there. Hold on."

He dove forward through the door, falling into a rolling motion. Four shots fired. He came up out of the roll, aimed, and placed two rounds into the man standing at the front door. The second lay on the ground, dead. Looking around, he saw Eden standing in the doorway with her gun.

"We better call the cops," Tom said.

"Let's make sure there are no more of them first," she replied.

They systematically checked the rest of her apartment for more intruders, but didn't find any. They did hear the distant sound of sirens approaching, and Eden suggested they get ready.

"They must've followed me somehow," Tom said.

She looked shocked. "You?'

"Maybe having something to do with my mission in Afghanistan." He turned his gaze on her and narrowed his eyes. "Or was it you they were after?"

Eden shifted her weight from foot to foot.

Tom's eyes widened. "It was *you* they were after. You weren't kidding when you said it wasn't safe for me to date you."

"Told ya," she said, slipping a pair of running pants on, commando.

"This is serious. You can't keep this from me." He donned his shirt.

"The hell I can't."

He grabbed her by the arm. "If you're in danger, I wanna know. I need to know. I can't leave you to these assholes. You need protection."

"I manage," she bit out, jerking her arm from his grasp. She fastened her bra and pulled a sweater over her head.

"Really? And how would you have taken out these assholes if I hadn't been here?"

"Of course, you were great, but I could have held my own."

"Not without injury, maybe serious."

"Maybe." She shifted her gaze away from his piercing stare.

Tom buttoned up his shirt and stuffed it in his pants. "We don't have much time. Tell me," he demanded, fastening his belt.

"I can't. Won't. You need to walk away. Safe. I want you safe." She blinked twice and took a breath.

"What about you? You think I'm going to leave you defenseless?"

"I'm not exactly defenseless." Eden shoved her feet in boots.

"Crap. You've got a God damn arsenal in here, but you're alone."

"That's right. And now, you know why."

"I don't. Not all of it. Come clean." He slipped on his shoes and tied them.

There was a loud bang on the door. "Police. Open up."

"Too late," she said. "Cops."

"I'm not leaving you." His mouth set in a grim line.

Eden smiled at him and grasped his forearm. "Thank you. But one of us needs to stay alive."

"Both of us. I'm not leaving."

"Bless you, Davis."

Before she could utter another word, the police broke through the door. They came in with guns drawn. By now, Tom and Eden sat at the kitchen table. The scent of fresh coffee permeated the room. Eden pushed to her feet, heading for the cabinet and a second pair of mugs. Two dead, masked men in black lay on the floor next to their weapons.

"Hold it right there," the officer in charge said to Eden as he aimed his firearm at her. She turned to face him. Tom stood. They raised their empty hands, palms forward, to show the cops that they were unarmed.

"Get on the ground!" one of them yelled.

Tom and Eden slowly, but immediately, dropped to their knees then to the floor, palms down.

The first cop put his knee on Tom's lower spine, grabbed his wrists, pulling them behind his back, and handcuffed him. After Tom was cuffed, the officer did the same to Eden. Once they were both subdued, he yanked them up and sat them in chairs.

"Who are you?"

"Eden Wyatt, this is my apartment."

Using the radio microphone on his shoulder, he called in a request to dispatch as to who the resident of the address was. Confirming that it was Eden Wyatt, he asked her where her ID was. As his partner went to get it, he started questioning them.

"Ok, explain what happened here."

"These men broke in. We shot them. That's it," Eden replied.

"They're packing some pretty heavy stuff to be petty robbers. Who are they, and why did they break in?"

Eden shrugged, but Tom answered, "They were after me. They must've followed me here."

The cops wanted to know why they would be after Tom. He told them about Afghanistan and their mission—at least the declassified information. The whole time Tom spoke, Eden stared at him. Once the cops had confirmed the facts and established Eden's identity with the State Department, they uncuffed and released the pair.

"It'll take a few days for forensics to finish. Get what you need, and find another place to stay," the officer said.

By this time, residents of the building had gathered in the hall. Mick pushed through the crowd. "They can stay with us. We live upstairs."

The officer nodded and moved away to confer with his partner.

"Thanks Mick, but we can get a hotel room," Tom said.

"Ridiculous. Our sofa makes into a bed," Tara chimed in.

Eden blushed, but agreed.

The policeman returned. He handed her his card, wrote down her cell number on his notepad, and told her that he would call her when she could come back. She quickly grabbed a few things, Tom shouldered his duffel, and they left.

* * * *

Tara made an early lunch while the others sat around the table.
"What the hell happened down there?" Mick asked.
Tom nodded toward Eden. "Want to tell them?"
She shook her head. "Can't."
Tom shared the events that had occurred.
Tara passed out plates of sandwiches then sank down into a chair next to her husband. "Crap. Right downstairs? You two could have been killed." She shivered.
"Exactly. Which is why I want an explanation from Miss Eden, here, as to why. We need to know, so we can be prepared if it happens again." Tom picked up his ham and cheese.
"Sorry. Classified." Eden stuffed food into her mouth to prevent talking.
The day was spent at the movies. Initially afraid to leave the apartment, Eden gave in to Tom's assurance she'd be safe. She stayed vigilant, on high alert, all the way to the theater and back, ready to spring into action, if necessary.
The relief from fear for a few hours at the cinema renewed her. They returned to Mick and Tara's apartment, checked for the match when opening the door, and then ate Chinese take-out food. They retired early, making up the bed together in silence. The sofabed was much smaller than Eden's queen-sized bed. But she planned to sleep tucked into Tom's embrace like a nesting doll, so it didn't matter. When he closed his arms around her, peace flowed in her veins.
"You're gonna be okay. But it would be easier if you told me."
"I know, but I can't."
His response was a kiss on her cheek and the shielding of her thighs by his, folded up behind. Snuggling into his chest, she sighed and closed her eyes. Exhaustion from tension and fear quickly sent her into a restless sleep.
At midnight, Eden slipped out of bed without making a sound. She didn't want to disturb Tom or her friends. She perched her

bottom on the windowsill and looked out at the street below. Streetlights tried, unsuccessfully, to warm a portion of the frigid air around them. Her gaze scanned the area, looking for armed men tucked away in the shadows.

Her pulse jumped at the sudden appearance of a lone figure. He wore a hoodie pulled low over his forehead, his breath was visible. His head turned slightly from side to side. He appeared to be looking for something, before stopping at a garbage can and opening the lid. The light reflected off the shiny barrel of a gun. He put it in his pocket and moved away.

Eden shuddered. *Is he a thief? A mugger? Or is he after me?* In that instance, she knew she couldn't stay. *Every stranger is a terrorist, out for revenge. Every hooded figure is a murderer. Am I paranoid or destined to die here? I'm putting Mick and Tara in danger.*

She hardened her resolve to find another hiding place. The newlywed couple had been very good to her, and she wasn't about to thrust them in harm's way so that she could stay in New York City.

A noise caused her to spin around. She aimed the gun in her hand as she turned.

"You've got to stop pointing guns at me," Tom quipped, closing his strong fingers around her wrist and shoving it toward the floor. He removed the firearm with his other hand and put it on the table beside him.

"I'm sorry," she said, turning back toward the window. Tom moved up behind her, resting his hands on her shoulders. The heat from him penetrated the thin fabric of her nightgown, warming her skin.

"What are you doing up?" he asked.

"Why did you lie to the police?"

"I didn't lie. Those men might be after me."

"You know damn well I was their target." She played with the edging on the curtains.

"I didn't want to blow your cover. Figured I'd leave that up to you."

"I'm leaving tomorrow."

"Oh? Where are we going?"

"We? Did I say 'we'? I'm going and I'm going alone."

His fingers gripped her shoulders tighter. "I don't think so."

"I've already endangered your life once. I'm not going to do it again."

"I'll decide that for myself."

She faced him. "Look, you got laid. Isn't that enough?" Grateful for the shadows masking her features, Eden steeled herself for his reply.

"Is that all it was to you?"

"That's all it was to you."

Tom chuckled. "You keep telling me where I'm not going and what I'm not feeling. What the hell?"

"You can drop all the Mr. Honorable shit now. I'm not mad that you only wanted to get laid. So did I. Now, we're both happy. And you go your way, and I go mine." She closed her mouth, hoping she'd stopped before the quiver in her voice gave her away.

"Remember your rule—no one-night stands? It wasn't a one-night stand to me."

"Oh yeah?" She cocked an eyebrow at him. "Are you saying it was love? Don't be ridiculous."

"Never met a woman like you before, Eden. I don't know what the hell it was…is. But it isn't over. Not by a long shot."

"Says you. What about me? Do you think I feel the same?"

"Let's find out." He took her in his arms and kissed her hard, taking her breath away. She made a motion to shove him away, but he ignored it. His hands on her back pressed her closer, and she melted against his bare chest. When he raised his head, his eyes glowed in the moonlight streaming through the window.

Eden sucked in a breath. *He's so handsome and so loving.*

"I'll decide if and when I leave. And where I go. Not you. I've spent one helluva long time, looking for a woman like you. No terrorist or asshole with a gun is going to drive me away."

Eden tried to hide a smile. "Tough guy, huh?"

"What do you think?"

"I think I love you, Davis."

He blew out a breath. "Back to Davis again?"

She chuckled then pushed up on her tiptoes and kissed him, pressing against his chest.

His hands closed on her hips before he moved away. "You starting something?" He cocked an eyebrow at her.

"Not here."

"Let's get a hotel room." He slid his hands up and down her arms.

"Not in New York. It's not safe. We have to leave."

"First, tell me what the hell's going on."

"Maybe."

He led her back to bed. Once they were lying down, Tom buried his face in her neck, planting sweet, sexy kisses. Eden squirmed.

"You can't expect me to be in bed with you and leave you alone."

"I was hoping you'd say that." She arched up to meet his kiss. When they broke, she bounced on the bed. Tom shot her a questioning glance. "Testing for squeaks."

He laughed. "Let's see how quiet we can be."

Eden slipped off her nightgown and snuggled underneath him. He glanced at the closed bedroom door once before turning his attention to her.

"Okay, L.C. Take me to the moon."

"My pleasure."

Chapter Six

Morning sun peeped into the living room, stabbing Tom in the eye. He rolled over, unwilling to leave the warmth of the bed or the embrace of the woman he loved. *Damn. How could I fall so fast? Didn't see her coming. She needs me, though she'd never admit it.*

She stirred, letting go, rolling over, away from him, and then inching closer while still sleeping. He pulled her against him. His body reacted to her soft rear end pressing into his groin. *Not now. No time. No privacy.*

But he couldn't resist her. The faint scent of her lilac perfume teased his nose. He brushed his lips across her neck. She moaned, but didn't open her eyes. Tom pulled the covers up over her bare shoulder and settled his hand on her breast before he closed his eyes again. She sighed and cuddled into him, her breathing returning to a steady rhythm.

He wanted to clear his mind, to focus on the love growing in his heart and the beautiful woman in his bed. But doubts crept in. His training couldn't be denied. It filled his head with questions. *Who is she? Why is she in danger? Who's trying to kill her? What is she hiding from me? Has she killed someone?* His body rested peacefully while his mind raced. He needed answers before he'd give his heart free rein to adore her.

A creak from a hinge drew his attention. The bedroom door opened, and Tara crept out on tiptoe. She wore a fluffy, light blue robe and padded barefoot to the bathroom. Tom realized Eden was naked and couldn't simply bound out of bed. He plucked her nightgown off the chair and laid it on the pillow next to her head.

For a moment, he abandoned his questions and recalled their second steamy night together. As he ran through their quiet lovemaking in his mind, his thumb caressed the soft skin of her breast.

He smiled at the memory that such a hot, sassy babe could be so soft and tender. Her sensual response to his kisses and his touch made him shiver. Her smooth skin, sweet scent and snug fit made his groin tighten.

When they were entwined, her gentle, loving expression won his heart. She was a mysterious mix of everything he wanted in a partner. *As long as she's fighting for our side, I'm okay.* Doubt marred the beauty of their intimate moments. *We have to clear this up today.*

He sat up and stroked her shoulder. "Hey, beautiful. Wake up. Rise and shine."

Eden turned over to face him. She cracked open her baby blues and smiled. "You're better than any sleeping pill invented." She yawned, covering her mouth with her hand.

"You mean I bore you to oblivion?"

She cocked an eyebrow. "Fishing for compliments? You know damn well I mean that you're a great lover."

He laughed. "That's better."

"Do we have to get up?" She snaked one arm around his middle.

"Have to get you to safety."

All at once, the memory of the day before spurred her to action. "Damn straight. Let's go." She snatched her nightie from the pillow and abandoned the bed. Tom followed.

Within half an hour, everyone was dressed. Tara fried up eggs. Mick tended bacon while Eden made toast. Tom set the table. When the food was ready, they ate in silence, passing the salt and the jam, but focusing on their breakfast and making little eye contact.

"Time to talk about the elephant in the room," Tom said, polishing off his toast.

"Like why those guys broke in and tried to kill you two? Yeah. What the hell was that about?" Mick scooped up his last forkful of eggs.

All eyes were on Eden. Tom watched her blush. *I need the truth.*

"Yes, they were after me, not Tom. No, I can't tell you why." She finished her bacon.

"If you want us to help you, we need to know what's going on," Tom said, placing his hand on her forearm.

"The more you know, the worse it'll be for you." Eden wiped her mouth with a napkin.

"We can take care of ourselves," Mick said.

Eden looked down at her hands.

"We're waiting." Tara stacked the plates.

"This is so beyond classified...but you sort of have a right to know."

Tara squeezed Eden's hand. "You can trust us."

Eden glanced at her mug.

Tom pushed to his feet and refilled everyone's coffee. "Okay. No more excuses."

Eden sighed.

* * * *

"I'm CIA. I was involved with Jerry, another agent. We'd grab weekends when we could, which wasn't very often. We were in love. Seriously. Talking marriage." She glanced at Tom. His expression was concerned, but not obviously upset about her previous relationship.

"We were having a beautiful, stolen weekend in Beirut. Jerry had finished a mission, and I was between assignments, too." She took a deep, shuddering breath.

Tom slid his fingers over hers. Eden looked up into his eyes.

"We were in bed. Lying there. They broke in. I don't know who they were, but I'd guess they were from Jerry's mission or relatives of the people killed. They burst through the door and shot Jerry...in the head. Right in front of me." Eden gasped as the memory flooded back. Her eyes watered.

Tom squeezed her hand.

She took a sip of her coffee and blew her nose.

"What happened next?" Mick asked, softly.

"They didn't know I was CIA. They thought I was only his girlfriend. So they took me. I ended up in the house of the brother of the man Jerry had killed."

"Oh, my God." Tara covered her mouth with her hand.

"Were you captive long?"

"About a week." Eden closed her eyes for a second.

"Were you tortured...or worse?" Tara asked in a whisper.

"I was beaten and almost raped. Thank God for my period." Eden chuckled bitterly. "My grandmother came over and went undercover in a bakery. She made poison muffins. They sent me with an armed guard to buy food. She told me which one was safe. I fed the doctored ones to the guards. They died quickly. I grabbed a gun and shot the Emir."

There was silence while Eden took a gulp of coffee.

"Gram and I took off. We slipped back into the States, undetected. Or so I thought. I know his relatives are looking for me. Those families are tight. Revenge is a necessary thing. It's taken for granted." Eden played with her spoon, tapping it on the table.

"How did they find you?" Tom asked.

"I don't know. But I need to move…alone."

"We've been over this. I'm going with you." Tom shifted in his chair.

"I'm going on assignment about the time your leave is over."

"We'll be together until then."

"But…"

"No buts. It's a done deal. I'm staying with you." Tom trapped her hand under his, and gazed into her eyes.

Eden sighed. "You win. Now, we need to find a place to go."

"How about St. Thomas?" Tara piped up.

"I have a place there. A house. Not far from the beach, but—" Tom began.

"Nice place. Perfect," Mick said, downing the rest of his beverage.

"But it's rented. I've got tenants there for four months," Tom finished.

"How about our place, then?" Mick asked.

"Yeah. My mom was there, but she came back on Wednesday." Tara gathered up the mugs.

"Also in St. Thomas?" Eden asked. Tara nodded.

Eden looked at Tom. He raised his eyebrows. "Might work. The island has limited access."

"First, a trip to the drugstore. That golden hair has got to go," Tara said, rising from her seat.

"Yep. Let's go." Eden and Tara put on their coats and headed out the door.

They walked side-by-side for a block before Tara spoke. "I know it's none of my business, but are you in love with Tom?"

"I guess so. He snuck under my radar."

"That was pretty fast."

"I've been alone a long time. Sorta developed a sixth sense for creeps. Haven't met anyone like him since...Jerry, I guess."

"Do you want to get married?"

"I thought Davis and I'd have some fun until he had to leave, but something happened. It clicked. I trust him. I haven't trusted anyone...for a long time." Eden smiled.

"So, you *are* in love?"

"Yeah. It's weird. We're so alike. And he's so sexy." Eden sensed a blush in her cheeks.

"Mick, too." Tara reddened. "I mean...we're very compatible."

"Oh? He's not sexy?" Eden tried to hide a grin.

"Well, I mean..." Tara's color deepened. "Yeah. Very sexy. But not something I usually talk about."

"We're more women of action than talk."

Tara hit her friend playfully in the shoulder and laughed.

"Be careful. I'm a trained fighter," Eden chuckled.

"I'm not afraid of you." Tara shot a smirk at her friend.

They entered the store and went right to the hair dye section. They picked up different boxes and discussed the colors. Tara held one up to Eden's face.

"This shade goes well with your coloring."

"Autumn chestnut. A little bit of red. Do you think it's too close to blonde?" Eden turned the package over in her hand.

"Can't use black. Too dramatic. Black'll bring more attention to you, not less," Tara said.

"Do they have one labeled 'mousy brown'?" The women laughed. "Okay. Autumn chestnut, it is."

"Are you sad to be leaving blonde behind?" Tara asked as she strolled toward the check-out.

"Not really. Won't have to put up with dumb blonde jokes in bars. Hope Davis likes it."

"I'm sure he'll like you in anything."

"Or nothing."

The women giggled as they entered the apartment. Eden pulled the box out of the bag and marched over to the lieutenant colonel.

"Well? What do you think?"

Tom took it then glanced at her. "You're beautiful no matter what color your hair is. This might be…uh…very…exciting?"

Eden wiggled her eyebrows at him, making him blush. "Giving you ideas?"

"Hell, yeah." He laughed.

"Come on, Eden." Tara tugged on her friend's sleeve. "I'll help you."

"Mick and I are making plans to leave late this afternoon," Tom said, leaning down to brush his lips against hers.

"Good. The sooner, the better."

* * * *

When Eden had finished blowing her hair dry, Tom reported the results of his reconnaissance.

"I checked downstairs. There are still a couple of forensic people, but they said you could get some of your stuff."

Eden tiptoed around the lab people taking samples and pictures. She grabbed a suitcase in the bedroom closet she had packed in case of an emergency. It was a large overnight bag and held everything she'd need for a month or longer. She smiled to herself. *Always knew planning ahead would come in handy.*

"We'll probably be finished by morning," a forensic tech said.

Eden nodded and returned to Mick and Tara's.

"Change of plans. We're staying the night and leaving in the morning," Tom said when she closed the front door.

"Damn. Can't leave sooner?"

He shook his head. "Flights are booked. It's only one night."

Eden cozied up to him, snaking her arms around his middle. "One more night here with you? Being quiet? Oohhh, love the challenge."

He chuckled and lowered his mouth to hers.

"Who are the newlyweds around here?" Mick said, grinning. Tom and Eden parted as he mumbled something. Mick laughed. "You two are worse than we are."

Eden spent the afternoon watching out the window with binoculars while Mick and Tara packed. They ordered in food and watched a chick flick to calm jumpy nerves. At ten, they parted for the night.

Eden and Tom slipped naked under the sheets.

"Your hands are cold," she said.

Tom rubbed them together then placed them under his armpits to warm his fingers. Eden snuggled up to him, kissing his chest and running her nails over his lower back.

"Damn, that's good," he muttered. He freed his hands, closing them around her, drawing her into his embrace.

The skin-to-skin contact turned her on. She nestled her cheek into his chest. His masculine scent soothed her. Fear temporarily moved out of her thoughts while lust took over. She hitched her leg over his waist.

Need rose up inside Eden like a hungry panther. She wanted him now and refused to think about the future. He glided his hand down her back to rest on her rump.

"Your body is perfect."

"Nothing about me is perfect."

"Stop arguing."

"Aye, aye, sir. Kiss me."

"My kind of orders," he said, bending his head down to reach her lips.

Eden opened for him, and he devoured her. His desire was clearly as strong as hers. The fire running through her veins made every inch of her skin tingle as it came in contact with his. She surrendered to him, following his lead. And he didn't disappoint. He entered her, and their bodies rocked. Neither commented on noise. They took each other with a need born of love mixed with fear.

Eden clamped her mouth on his shoulder as heat bubbled up and over into an intense orgasm. Her hips undulated with his as he stepped up the pace. Before long, he groaned into her hair, his hands closing over her shoulders in a vise-like grip.

Pleasure filled her as her panting subsided. Her fingers caressed his back, sliding through a sheen of sweat. A grin stretched her lips as a sigh escaped her throat.

"Something wrong?" he whispered.

"Everything's so right."

He rolled off, letting cold air cover her where his body had been before. She shivered, and he pulled up the blankets. He kissed her sweetly. She cupped his cheek.

"You're amazing, D—Tom."

She swore she could feel him smile. "Tom. I like the way you say it."

"Don't let go, okay?"

"All night?"

"All night."

"You got it." He eased her over on her side and tucked his knees up under hers. When he folded his arm over her, she kissed it and covered his hand with hers.

Eden closed her eyes. "Good night, L.C."

"Good night, beautiful."

Eden awoke tangled up with him. Legs and arms wound around each other. She giggled then kissed his neck and blew in his ear. He grimaced, frowned, and stared down at her.

"Good morning, Davis."

"Davis..." he grumbled.

"Okay, okay. Good morning, handsome, sexy, adorable Tom."

He cocked an eyebrow. "Adorable?"

"I *am* a girl, you know."

"Hell, yeah, you bet I know." And he started to laugh.

Eden unwound from him with a sigh, sad to leave the shelter of his body.

The bedroom door opened, and Mick came out wearing a robe. "Time to get up, lovebirds," he snickered.

"We're not fooling around. Only trying to unwind," Eden said.

"Sure, sure. I've heard that before." Mick chuckled.

"Damn. My robe is across the room."

Tom swung his legs over the side. He retrieved it and returned in a couple of long strides.

"My hero," she cooed, smiling.

"We need to get going. Plane leaves at eleven hundred hours," Mick said, checking his watch.

Eden was the first one dressed. She stood at the door with her suitcase when her cell phone rang.

"It's Sergeant Michaels. You can go back into your apartment now," he said, then hung up.

"Good news," she called out. "I can get back into my place. I'm going to stop down there and grab a couple of things I forgot. Meet you in front."

"I'm almost ready—" Tom began.

Eden stopped his words with a serious kiss. She gripped his middle and kissed him hard. "Don't hurry. I'll only be a minute." She stopped for a second at the door and stared at him.

Tom smiled at her and continued to button his shirt.

She clutched her bag and descended the stairs fast. After entering her apartment, she opened the first closet and fished an HK Compact Tactical .45 out of a secret hiding place in the rear, checked it for ammo, and tucked it under her arm. The windows facing the fire escape were broken. The remaining glass had been removed. She leaned out, tossed her bag down to the street, cocked her gun, and held it in front. Nimbly, she climbed down the ladder and jumped to the sidewalk.

As soon as she picked up her suitcase, two men appeared from around the corner. They started firing at her. Eden blasted back. She hit one shooter in the leg, and he went down. The other pulled back behind the building.

Eden took off down the empty street. The armed man chased after her. She pivoted and squared off. She steadied the gun in both hands and kept firing at him until he went down. Then, she dropped the weapon down the storm drain and disappeared into the subway.

* * * *

Tom heard the shots. "Eden!"

He and Mick ran out of the apartment. Tom tossed one of Eden's spare guns to his buddy as they fairly flew down the stairs. They entered the empty apartment cautiously, Tom pushing the door open with one hand while brandishing the gun with the other.

Only silence greeted them. A quick check in the rooms and closets established there were no gunmen. They went to the window. Tom called Eden's name down the street, but got no reply.

They heard sirens in the distance and spotted one man limping badly toward the subway. The other lay on the sidewalk, in a pool of blood, not moving.

"We'd better get out of here before the cops come. We've got a plane to catch," Mick said.

He and Tom exited in a hurry. Tara was standing in the hallway with the suitcases beside her when they returned. Within five minutes, they had their luggage and were racing down the street. Tara spied a cab, and they jumped in as the police car screeched to a stop. Mick peered out the back window, but the cops weren't following them. The sound of doors slamming announced the arrival of more officers. Still, none looked in their direction. Mick blew out a breath.

"Where's Eden?" Tara asked.

"She said she didn't want me to go with her," Tom replied.

"Guess she meant it," Mick said.

"So, then, where is she?"

Tom shrugged. "Flew the coop." Beads of sweat broke out on his forehead.

The atmosphere in the taxi was tense. Tara broke the silence again. "Maybe she's meeting us at the terminal."

Tom shot her a sharp look. "Do you really think so?"

"I don't, but I thought maybe you did?"

"She's gone. She said she wouldn't drag me into this. I should've known she was too stubborn to listen to reason. We've got to find her. She's out there alone."

"She sure as hell isn't staying in New York," Mick put in.

"Who knows how many others are hunting her down?" Tom said, the worry in his voice almost palpable.

Mick put his hand on Tom's forearm. "We'll find her."

Tom turned to Tara. "Do you have any idea where she'd go?"

"Me? No. She never talked much about traveling. I don't think she has much family, either."

"Damn it," Tom muttered.

"Wait. She used to talk about running off to Montana. She had a couple of pictures of Montana ranches on her computer. Said such big country was the perfect place to disappear."

"What airlines fly to Montana?"

Mick whipped out his phone.

A tiny spark of hope grew in Tom's heart. *You can't get away from me so easy, beautiful. I'm never going to let you go. Hang on. I'm on my way.* He chewed on a fingernail while Mick checked the airlines.

"There are three. Western Air, Liberty, and Green Airways."

Tom leaned over to the cab driver. "Forget Caribbean Sun. Take us to Liberty Airlines instead."

"Are you sure? How do you know it's Liberty?" Tara asked.

"Because she's CIA," Tom whispered.

Mick chuckled. "Good point."

Tom sat back in his seat. He thanked God traffic was light. The taxi sped up First Avenue to the RFK Bridge. His mind was too preoccupied for him to take in any sights as the car drove through Queens. Medium-sized gray buildings appeared to fly by his window, but Tom didn't notice. All he could think about was the danger Eden was in. He refused to play out what would happen if one of the gunmen caught up with her.

He took out a handkerchief and mopped the sweat off his forehead. *She's smart. She'll give them the slip.*

"We'll find her," Tara said.

"And when we do, I'll take her over my knee..."

"Hey, TMI, Tom. If you're kinky, I don't need to know about it." Mick snickered, holding up his hands.

Tom laughed. "Leave it to you to say that."

"What are friends for?"

"Are you mad?" Tara asked.

Tom shook his head. "Not really. I understand her reasons."

"Maybe she did it because she loves you."

He turned to face her. "You think so?"

"Why else would she turn down help from someone like you?"

"Guess you're right. If that's true, all the more reason for me to be with her."

Tara smiled at him. "Glad to hear you say that."

"Love can be a two-way street, you know."

Tara glanced at Mick. "Oh, yes. I know that very well."

Chapter Seven

Eden blew out a breath when the subway doors closed. She rode uptown then switched trains to ride downtown, in case anyone was following her. She watched the passengers before transferring to a bus to the airport. Feeling naked without her gun, she searched her purse for a makeshift weapon and smiled when she discovered a compact with a mirror. *Worst case, I can smash the mirror and use the pieces as a knife. If I don't slice myself to ribbons along the way.*

She leaned back and looked out the window as the bus pulled onto the highway. The sky was a blanket of gray. Rain threatened. *Or maybe snow?* She zipped her down jacket up all the way to protect against the bit of cold air leaking in through the cracks. She shivered. *If Tom was here, I could snuggle up to him for warmth. And protection. At least he'll stay safe. Bet he's pissed I gave him the slip.* She grinned.

The smile melted off her face as she wondered if she'd ever see him again, ever feel his touch. Her heart ached when she thought about him. She pictured him standing tall, dress uniform, medals...the handsomest man in the world. Then in bed, naked, his broad shoulders looming over her. Her pulse kicked up at the images. She yearned for the grasp of his hand, the reassurance from his eyes that everything was going to be all right.

But everything wasn't going to be all right. *Stupid idiot. Why did you fall for him? What a jerk. You think you can have a life like everyone else? You can't. Face it. Accept it. Deal with it.* She stared out the window at the old, dirty, gray buildings. The sight depressed her. *People who live there have lives. They fall in love, marry, have children. They don't spend their days hiding. I don't want to do it anymore. I have a right to a life.*

Her mind raced, searching for a way out of the maze of running, hiding, and fear she lived in. Then, she thought of a solution. *The only way I can move forward is to take these people out. I have to kill them before they kill me.*

The bus stopped at Liberty Airlines. She got out and pulled out her cell phone. She hauled her bag a hundred feet away from the structure and dialed. While she waited for the call to go through, her gaze searched the people milling about, getting to their flights. Her hand closed around the compact hidden in her purse.

"Sumner, please." She leaned against the building, feeling more comfortable knowing her back was protected.

"That you, Eden?" A raspy, female voice greeted her.

"Yeah. Hi."

"You're still in one piece? Thank God."

"Thanks, Lynn. Is he in?"

"Sure. I'll connect you."

"Eden. You're amazing. How the hell do you do it?" She heard a smile in his deep tone.

"I'm not doing it anymore," she blurted out. *Way to be subtle and persuasive, idiot.*

"What?"

"Whatever mission you had for me, cancel it."

"Why?"

"I have a new mission."

"You do?"

"Yeah. I'm gonna get these guys before they get me. The best defense is a good offense."

"You can't do that. There are more of them than there are of you."

"I can outsmart them."

"Unlikely. No offense. You're outnumbered."

"But if you gave me a team, I'll bet we could get them."

"A team? You want a team? For a personal vendetta?"

"Do you want me to stay with the Agency?"

"Of course, I do."

"I can't do that hiding out all the time. We have to get rid of them. They are a cancer in my life, in the world. I want to blast them into oblivion."

There was silence.

Eden's resolve began to slip. Tears pricked at the back of her eyes. "Please, Sumner. I want to get my life back. The Agency has to assume some responsibility for this."

"Okay. Let me see what I can do. You still have ten days to think about this."

"I won't change my mind."

He sighed. "I don't know if I can pull this off, but I'll try. I'd hate to lose you."

"That makes two of us."

Sumner's tone softened. "He must be pretty special."

"Who?" Eden pretended ignorance.

"The man you want to be with."

"He is." She smiled.

"Take care of yourself. Let us know where you land."

"Will do."

"Be safe."

Eden closed her phone and headed for the terminal.

* * * *

The cab pulled up to the curb in front of Liberty Airlines at LaGuardia Airport. Tom and Mick took the bags. The three entered the doors and stopped. The terminal was teeming with people. Families with children, senior citizens, single people, all milling around, looking for their gates, changing their tickets, begging to get on sold-out flights.

"Let's split up," Mick suggested.

"Damn. That new hair color'll make her blend in," Tom said.

"We'll find her," Tara said.

They divided up the area between the two men. Mick was assigned to check out the gate to the flight they guessed she was on while Tara hawked every ladies' restroom. They fanned out. The first place Mick went, there was a plane scheduled for Butte. But it wasn't leaving for two hours, and he didn't see Eden there.

Tom tried to be inconspicuous, but in full uniform it wasn't easy. He was stopped by people who had sons or boyfriends in the military. He chatted with them for a moment then begged off, saying he was looking for a friend.

Tara checked in with Mick and Tom when she had established that Eden wasn't hiding in either of the two bathrooms. Time ticked away. The threesome went to the computer bar and faced away from the gate.

"We have to wait here and hope we've picked the right place," Tom said. They ordered coffee and sipped while they watched the hands of the clock slowly tick away the seconds.

Mick was the first to spot her. She had a scarf tied around her hair.

"That her?" he asked Tom, pointing.

Tom's head snapped around quickly. He recognized the seductive sway of her rear end and blew out a breath. "Yes. That's her. Thank God."

Eden looked around, causing the trio to hide by turning their backs to her. The flight attendant began calling rows. They saw Eden pace.

"I've got an idea." Tom put his bag down next to his friend.

"Go for it," Mick said.

"Darling!" Tom called, running up to Eden. He grasped her upper arm firmly. "There you are. I've been looking all over for you. This is not our flight."

Eden glared at him.

Tom looked at the attendant. "She's pregnant and forgets everything. We've only been married two years and sometimes she forgets I'm her husband." He chuckled. "Come, sweetheart. Our plane is leaving, but at a different gate." He grinned at the woman in charge, who smiled back. Tom bent down and kissed Eden. "Don't bite me," he whispered.

She let him kiss her and shrugged at the agent. "Pregnancy. Who knew?"

She went along quietly with Tom, who continued his iron grip on her arm.

"Someone's been a bad girl," he said through clenched teeth.

"Are you going to punish me?" she asked, walking fast to keep up with him.

"What do you think'd be fair?" he replied as they joined the others.

"Confine me to bed with you for a week," she answered, her eyes twinkling.

Tom burst out laughing.

Mick checked his watch. "We've got only twenty minutes to make our flight."

"Let's go." Tom looked at her. "I'm not letting go of you."

"I'll be good. I promise."

"Like I believe you. No way. You're coming with us. No discussion."

"Aye, aye." Eden saluted.

Tom glared at her. "You put me through hell this morning." He quickened his pace.

"I'm sorry. I did it to protect you." Eden was practically running to keep up with his long strides.

"Did you think I wouldn't come after you?"

"I didn't think you'd find me. How did you?"

"Tara."

Eden glanced behind at her friend, who shrugged.

"Did you think I didn't care about you? That I'd walk away?" Tom said, his jaw twitching.

"I thought you'd be safe." She steadied the bag on her shoulder.

"You can't get away from me. I'll never let you go." He laced his fingers with hers.

Eden's eyes watered. "Do you mean that?"

"I said it, didn't I?"

"I think I love you, Davis," she muttered.

"Davis…again."

"Tom. I mean Tom."

They reached the gate, and the attendant smiled. "We were looking for you."

She ushered them on board. They sat in two rows of two seats. Tom put Eden by the window.

"This way you're trapped. You can't disappear."

"I won't. I promise."

"I've heard that before."

"Honestly, Tom." She stroked his arm, raising her gaze to meet his.

"I hope you brought a bathing suit."

"I may have been heading for Montana, but I packed for St. Thomas."

"A bikini?"

"Of course," she said, lowering her voice and staring into his eyes.

"Whew. It's getting hot in here."

"Not nearly as hot as it's going to get, L.C." Eden leaned over and kissed him.

* * * *

The plane turned sharply, touched down, and then came to an abrupt halt on the short runway outside of Charlotte Amalie. Warm, moist air caressed the faces of the four friends as they walked to the terminal.

"It's beautiful," Eden said, glancing around. Behind them, the mountain, green with healthy vegetation, rose up on the far side of the aircraft, while the long, white stretch of beach beckoned to her on the other. "I've never been anyplace that had mountains and beach."

"It's a small island, but it has everything," Mick said.

Tom took Eden's hand again.

"Still don't trust me?" She squinted up at him.

"Nope."

She shook her head and gave a laugh. "You're a tough guy, Davis."

"Cautious."

"Come on. Mick's got us a taxi," Tara said, leading the way.

Eden enjoyed the ride to their place by the beach. She spied small, pastel-colored homes nestled among palm trees and grander ones tucked into the hills. She took a deep breath, expanding her lungs and filling them with gentle, moist, Caribbean air. Leaving winter behind refreshed her. *Until they catch up to me, I'm safe. Can I enjoy a day or two with the L.C. without being on guard? Maybe.*

"This is the land of lovers," Tara said. "Mick and I fell in love here."

Tom pulled Eden to him and kissed her head.

"It's beautiful here, Tara. I can see how easy it would be to fall in love," Eden said, glancing at Tom from under her lashes.

His gaze searched hers. "Do I need a leash?" he asked, cocking an eyebrow.

"Wow, no. I don't play those games." Eden chuckled. "But I might be persuaded to put on a skimpy maid's uniform."

"TMI, guys," Mick chimed in, covering his ears and laughing.

"That's not what I meant. You're avoiding the subject. Are you going to be good?" Tom tightened his grip on her hand.

"I'm always good, at least that's what men say." Eden snickered.

"Eden…"

She frowned. "Okay, okay. Fine. I'm not going to run away."

"Guys, can I trust her?" Tom glanced from Mick to Tara and back.

"Outside of handcuffs, I don't see what choice you have," Tara replied.

"Handcuffs? Oohh, kinky," Eden joked.

Mick and Tara carried their luggage into their room and closed the door.

Tom grabbed her upper arm hard and yanked her against his chest. "No more joking. No funny stuff. This isn't a game, Eden. It's your life."

"Joking is how I deal with this shit. If I get too serious, it freaks me out."

"You're not going to run away again, right?" Tom's brows creased, his jaw hard.

She looked up at him. "I won't. I promise."

"Good." He let her go. She rubbed her arm. "Sorry. I didn't mean to hurt you."

"Just a little uncomfortable. Takes a lot more to really hurt me." She turned away from him.

"Hey." He reached for her. She moved closer to him, and he drew her into his embrace, holding her gently. His whispered words were tender, "It's taken me a lifetime to find you. I'm not gonna let anything or anyone take you away."

She sighed, snaking her arms around him, resting against his chest. "You're the best, Tom."

The bedroom door opened. Tara and Mick, wearing bathing suits, emerged.

"I'm starving. Let's see what Mom left in the fridge." Tara padded into the kitchen.

"I'm going to change first. This is a tropical island. We need to blend in," Eden said, heading toward the guest room. Tom followed along with the suitcases. They claimed their sides of the bed and unpacked. Shyness seeped into Eden. *I've been naked with this man. Slept with him. Why am I reluctant to get undressed in front of him?*

"Excuse me." She plucked her bikini and cover-up from the suitcase and disappeared into the bathroom.

"Can you crack that door open?" Tom asked.

"Don't trust me?"

"Should I? Didn't you just run away?"

"Okay, okay. But don't come in." Eden stood by the crack, watching, as she slipped her suit over her bottom.

"You picked a helluva time to get shy, beautiful." Tom shed his uniform and donned trunks. He slipped a white T-shirt over his head. As he was hanging up his clothes, Eden opened the door all the way. She stood, fidgeting, in a turquoise bikini that left little to the imagination.

"Holy Hell," Tom muttered as his gaze swept her body.

She shifted her weight. "Like it?"

"Are you kidding? If Mick and Tara weren't waiting for us, I'd—"

"You'd what?" She shot him a flirtatious smile.

"Rip those scraps from your body and take you right now."

Her pulse kicked up. *He makes my blood pump.* "Open a window. It's warm in here." She fanned herself with her hand.

Tom chuckled as he turned the handle on the louvered windows. "You're a one-woman heat machine, baby."

"Hold that idea. Let's eat. I'm starved." She took his hand and headed for the kitchen.

Tom patted her behind once before they went through the doorway.

* * * *

Eden held on to the lieutenant colonel as Mick steered the car down the left side of the street. She placed her hand over her eyes more than once when they whizzed around a corner. Tom laughed at her panic.

"You haven't been to London?"

"That's England. I'd expected that."

"You didn't know St. Thomas is the same?"

She shook her head. "It's a big surprise."

"I've been driving here for a while, Eden. Don't worry," Mick said.

"He's a great driver," Tara put in.

Eden squeezed Tom's hand.

"It's okay, baby," he whispered.

Mick parked the car, and Eden was the first one out. Tom had a little trouble squeezing his large frame out of the tiny vehicle. The foursome roamed the stalls, and shops in Charlotte Amalie. Tom and Eden bought hats, colorful shirts, and exotic liqueurs. They finished their day at a casual, open-air restaurant. Sipping piña coladas, they planned their strategy.

"Eden and I have nine days left on leave," Tom said.

"You think you can find these guys then?" Mick questioned, draining his glass.

"Nope. I'm hoping to lure them here," Tom replied.

"How can we do that if they don't know where I am?" Eden asked.

"Good question. We need to map this out."

They finished their dinner, chatting about other topics. Eden relaxed a bit after a couple of drinks. Steel drum music lured them onto the dance floor, and they escaped their cares with the swing of their hips and the movement of their feet.

Back at the house, they bid goodnight and each couple adjourned to their room. Eden washed up, undressed, and joined Tom in bed. He flipped the light off. The sound of tropical insects and the faint crashing of gentle waves on the shore filled the air.

When she snuggled up to him, Tom put his arm around her shoulders. "Have you ever wondered how those people knew where you were?"

"Are you kidding?" She sat up. "I've spent days wondering how they knew where Jerry was, and if they did, why didn't they know who I was? I've gone around and around on it."

"But this last attack. That's new. How'd they know exactly where you were?"

"There are only two people who I've talked to in the Agency since I moved to New York."

"And they are?"

"My immediate superior, who I'll call I.S. because I'm not supposed to give out his name, and his secretary, Lynn."

"Are their lines secure?"

"I don't know. Who knows when something is written down and left on a desk and who else sees it? Or if someone has tapped the phone?"

"Tell me about these two."

"Let's see. I.S. is a guy, about forty-five years old. I think he's always had a crush on me, but it's hard to tell."

Tom frowned. "Did he ever make a pass at you?"

"Not exactly. He's joked around sometimes about us ending up together. You know, kinda like—'When the smoke clears, Eden, you and I'll be the only ones left. That's okay with me.'"

Tom nodded. "Go on."

"And yeah, I might have flirted back…a little bit."

"Really?" He raised his eyebrows.

"I get lonely."

He bent down to brush her lips with his. "Not when I'm around."

"Nope." She cuddled up to him, snaking her arm around his middle and resting her head on his shoulder.

"Go on," he prompted again.

"To be honest, maybe a little more than flirting. But it's been over for a long time with I.S."

"What about Lynn?"

"Lynn? She's like a second mother. Her daughter, Rosemary, and I were close friends. Lynn used to invite me for holiday dinners at their house. Rosie and I went out to bars a couple of times, looking for guys." Eden's eyes watered.

"What?"

"She started dating someone. Wouldn't tell me who it was. I lost her friendship. I think she was afraid he'd like me better than her, or that I'd try to take him away or something. But I'd never do that. I'm a loyal friend."

"Of course." He kissed her hair. "So, what happened?"

"Something went wrong. Maybe it was with this guy…I don't know. Rosie committed suicide. She jumped off the Key Bridge in D.C."

"Terrible."

"It was. Her mother took it hard. She went on a leave for six months. After that, we became real close. It was almost like I was her replacement for Rosemary."

"You're still close?"

"Yep. I trust her with my life."

"You trust both of them with your life, whether you want to or not."

"True. I can't imagine what they would gain by having me killed."

"By now, I think it's the relatives of the guy you killed in Lebanon who are after you. But I still want to know how they found you in Manhattan."

"That's bugs me, too." Eden chewed on a nail.

"Does anyone besides the four of us know you're here?"

"No. I haven't even told Gram. But I.S. asked me to check in."

"There's a leak somewhere. Until we know where it is, don't check in with anyone."

"No one?"

"Go off the grid. That's the only way we can be certain you're safe."

She smiled. "Kinda appeals to me. Off the grid. Hiding from everyone…except you."

He touched her cheek. "I need to keep you safe. Let's have our few days together without looking for gunmen behind trees."

"It would be so great. I could live my life and not worry, not check closets or stop and turn around unexpectedly."

"Yep." He combed his fingers through her long hair. "And we'll be together."

"With Mick and Tara, too."

"Of course. Still, they're totally trustworthy."

"But we do need to tell them not to tell anyone I'm here."

"Right. First thing in the morning. Don't worry. Mick knows, and he'll tell Tara."

Eden blew out a breath. "Wow, it's so weird."

"What?"

"Not being afraid, alert. Being completely safe. It's been years."

"Who says you're safe?" He rolled onto his side. Eden started, so he stroked her back. "I mean—from a big, bad wolf like me?"

"Oh? Whew. For a minute, I thought…"

"You thought I'm here to kill you?"

"Stranger things have happened."

"I'm here to love you," he whispered.

"Tell me more." She snuggled down, flattening her palm against the hard muscle of his chest.

"I'd rather show you," he said, curling his fingers around her breast. She uttered a soft moan at his touch. Tom leaned over and captured her mouth with his. Eden wound her arms around his shoulders and pressed her hips against him.

"I see the motor's already running," she mumbled in his ear.

"Always is around you."

She ran her hands down then up his chest as he squeezed her flesh. Eden tilted her chin toward him. He bent his tall, strong body to reach her mouth. She opened for him, and their tongues danced. Her muscles tensed as she reached down to touch him. His masculine scent joined with the exotic fragrance of the air, luring her into submission, relaxing her into surrendering her heart along with her body.

Tom glided his hand down and over her rump. He stopped to cup her rear before continuing down between her legs. She tightened her grip on him when he stroked her warm, wet flesh.

"Take it easy down there."

"Sorry. Too strong?"

"A mite."

Eden loosened her grasp and moved her hand to his thigh. Leaning back, she closed her eyes and focused on the sensations he was creating with his fingers.

"Oh, God, Tom. Don't stop. Oh, baby, don't stop."

He eased one finger inside her, and her hips bucked up. She arched her back, pushing her breasts into his chest. Flames licked at her insides as an ache to have him grew. She groaned his name, and he chuckled in her ear.

"Now, you remember my name."

"Damn straight. God, Tom. Don't play with me."

"But you're so much fun to play with." He zeroed in on her neck, kissing his way down her chest to her peak. He drew the hard bud into his mouth and sucked. Eden's hips rose slightly with the pressure. When he inserted a second finger, Eden thought she'd go through the roof.

"Damn it, do it. Take me. I'm gonna come."

"Do it, beautiful. Come for me."

As if he had pushed a button, the heat spiraling up inside her exploded. A fierce orgasm jolted her hips up off the bed as her muscles clenched and released. Pure pleasure poured through her veins, planting a huge smile on her face. She opened her eyes, catching Tom staring at her. A wave of shyness washed over her. *God, he's seen everything about me. I'm naked all the way to my bones.* She began to shiver.

"You're the most beautiful woman I've ever seen." Tom pushed to his knees. He snatched the condom off the nightstand and covered himself.

Eden reached down. "Crap, you're hard as steel."

"All the better to love you with, my dear."

Before she replied, he was inside her.

He bent his neck to rest his forehead on hers. "God, you feel good. So tight. So damn tight."

Tom began to move. Eden raised her legs. He took hold of one and ran his hand down the smooth skin. "So soft." He rested it on his shoulder and plunged in all the way, filling her.

"Damn," she muttered. She reveled in every thrust. Her fingers clutched his back, pressing into his muscle. She hooked her other leg around his waist. His passion stoked hers. She wanted him with every fiber of her being. And now that they were joined, she was happier than she had been in a long time. As he created more and more tension inside her, she shut off her mind and let her body lead. Another orgasm rippled through her.

As she gasped, Tom moaned and found his release. She watched as he closed his eyes and a red, sexual flush stole up his chest. A bit of sweat broke out on the back of his neck. Eden ran her nails over it and delighted when he shivered.

"Holy Hell," he whispered, freezing in position. "I love you, honey," he said, so softly she wasn't sure she'd heard right.

"What? What did you say?"

"I love you, you beautiful, smart-mouthed badass."

"You do? Well now. We're even."

He chuckled. "I guess we are." He slowly withdrew, making her sad for a moment. Then, he headed for the bathroom.

Eden lay back and grinned.

When he returned, she burrowed under his arm and rested her cheek on his chest. "How many more days of this, L.C?"

"Eight?"

"Eight days of heaven." She yawned and was asleep before he could reply.

Chapter Eight

Eden adjusted easily to the steady temperature of about eighty-three degrees. She donned a big, floppy, pink, straw hat and glamorous sunglasses. She wore one of two bikinis and her white, gauzy cover-up every day. Flip-flops protected her feet from hot sand. The warm, moist air, the salt water, and the constant, gentle sound of waves lapping on the shore brought peace to the undercover agent.

She spent every minute with Tom. He slathered on sunblock to protect his fair skin and advised Eden to do the same. After a slight burn in the first two days, she heeded his advice. Lazy days swimming, snorkeling, and reading on the beach ended in lovemaking every night. Tara never left Mick's side, either. He took them out in his boat. They cruised by the smaller islands, even passing the one where Mick and Tara had been stranded.

"That's the island where we fell in love."

"Speak for yourself. I think I was already in love with you before we got there."

She hugged him from behind as he manned the wheel. Her lips brushed his neck.

Eden had watched the newlyweds all week. *I want that. I want what they have.* She sighed as Tom sidled up to her, snaking his arm around her naked waist. She'd gotten used to his touch, and she leaned into him like a plant bends toward sunlight. He had become her energy source, the place where her happiness began. She didn't know how he had managed to get under her skin so quickly. She found it hard to believe they were on the same page about everything. Perhaps he didn't have to be in agreement with her on everything under the sun. Maybe what they had was strong enough to keep them together. She wondered how long he'd continue to love her. For however long it was, she'd be happy, content to be with him. She'd keep him in her heart forever, no matter what. Happiness, however brief, was a rare commodity in her life. She couldn't stop smiling.

Dangerous Love Lost & Found

As Tom and Mick dragged the boat ashore on a small island, Eden's cell rang. Tara picked up a water jug and a picnic basket while Eden answered her phone. It was Sumner.

"Hey. How are you?"

"Good," she replied.

"Where are you? You promised to check in."

"Yeah. I know. But I'm doing what you said."

"What's that?"

"I'm having a good time and forgetting about everything else."

"And that means me, too?"

"It means the Agency. There'll always be a special place in my heart for you." She swung her legs over the side of the boat and eased down into the shallow water.

"Same here."

"Gotta go. More good times. Your orders."

"Wait. Where are—" But Eden cut the connection. She stuffed the cell in the breast pocket of her shirt and waded into shore. The men were spreading a blanket while Tara unpacked the basket. Eden came up behind Tom.

He turned. "Who was that?"

"My I.S."

"And?" He cocked an eyebrow at her.

"Didn't tell him a thing. He can't GPS me, because this is a disposable phone. Got it in New York. I set my other up to automatically forward to this number and left it in Manhattan."

Tara passed a container of cut up mango to Tom. He removed a slice and held it up to Eden's mouth. She opened, and he fed it to her.

"Good. We're still safe."

He said "we." Gotta love that man. Eden pushed away all thoughts about what would happen when their days in paradise were finished. She refused to be depressed or sad and ruin this precious time. Tom appeared to be relaxed, too. She chuckled to herself.

"What's funny?" he asked, pulling her down on the blanket next to him. Mick ripped off a piece of French bread and passed it to Tom. Tara handed a package of soft cheese to her husband, who smeared some on the bread and fed it to his wife.

"Nothing."

"Come on. No secrets."

"Just noticing how relaxed you are." She tried to keep a straight face, but couldn't.

"In this air? With the sun and the surf? Who could be tense?" He spread cheese on a piece of bread and tore it in half, offering some to her. She took it. "What's funny about that?"

"Nothing." She took a bite.

"You're hiding something," he said, narrowing his eyes.

Eden could feel a blush steal into her cheeks.

"Give. Or do I have to tickle it out of you?" His face glowed with mischief.

"It's kind of private."

"Aw, come on. Now, you've got all of us interested," Mick said between bites.

"Yeah. I want to know, too," Tara chimed in.

Eden took a deep breath. She raised an eyebrow and peered at Tom. "Sure you want me to say this out loud?"

"Hell yeah. We've got no secrets." He indicated Mick and Tara.

"I was thinking that with this much sex, even the most nervous person in the world would be relaxed," Eden blurted out.

Tom's mouth fell open for a second before he started to laugh. Mick and Tara joined in.

"The charm of St. Thomas," Tara said.

"Hell, the air alone makes you horny," Mick added.

Tom was bright red. Eden wagged a finger at him. "You asked for it."

"I'm not embarrassed."

"Really?"

"Okay. Maybe a little. But with this air and this beautiful woman in my bed, hell, I'm only human."

Eden sensed the heat in her cheeks intensifying. She dropped her gaze to the mango chunks and cheese on the small plate in front of her. After they finished their meal, they went swimming and looked for unusual shells in the sand.

As they were packing up, Eden's cell rang again. This time it was Lynn.

"Sumner put you up to calling me?"

"It was my idea. I was worried about you. Are you all right?"
"Couldn't be better."
"That's wonderful. Where are you, sweetheart?"
"Off the grid, Lynn."
"But why?"
"Only way I can stay safe."
"You don't think Sumner or I would have anything to do with what's happened to you, do you?"
"Of course not. I'm not convinced our lines are secure. Gotta go."
"Wait. Wait. Please, tell me where you are in case we need to send help."
"I have all the help I'll need. Talk to you soon." Eden hung up over the protests of Sumner's secretary. A pang of guilt shot through her at the insensitive way she'd treated Lynn. *Should I have told her? I don't want her to worry. Sumner's got a crush on me. Best for him to be put on hold for a bit anyway.*

"Another I.S.?" Tom asked as he folded up the blanket.
"Nope. Secretary."
"Did you tell?"
"Nope." Eden put the trash in one bag.
"Great. We stay safe." With one arm, he roped her around the waist and pulled her to his bare chest for a passionate kiss.
"Picnics make you horny, Davis?"
"We're back to Davis?"
"Just wanted to see if you were paying attention."
"Honey, when you're around, I'm always at attention." His gaze caressed her body slowly, giving her chills.
"Quit stalling. Let's head home." She laced fingers with him as they headed back to the boat. Mick and Tara were making out while the motor idled.
"Attention, Sergeant Peterson," Tom barked.
Mick snapped his head away from his wife and glared at Tom, who was laughing.
"Payback is coming," Mick grumbled as he returned both hands to the wheel.
Tom pulled up the anchor and tossed it in before he gave Eden a leg up. Then, he hoisted himself up and in. Suddenly, Mick kicked the motor up and turned the wheel sharply. The boat sliced

through a wave, sending spray into the stern, soaking the lieutenant colonel. He yowled as the cool water hit his warm skin. Mick laughed and sped ahead.

Eden stood up, holding on to the side while the wind blew her hair. Tom shook off on her, making her jump at the shock. She laughed along with him. Happiness welled up in her chest as a grin stretched her lips. Tom closed his arms around her and rested his chin on her head. She backed up, snuggling into him, content to be together, no matter for how long.

* * * *

On cloudy days, Eden and Tom slept in, cuddling together. She didn't know which were better, the days spent with Tom or the nights. After the lovemaking, she slept well, nestled into his body. Although Mick had managed to purchase guns for them, she no longer kept hers under her pillow. A strong sense of security washed over her. She enjoyed every moment.

One glance in the mirror told her the L.C. was good for her. Her skin was wrinkle-free, clear, and smooth. She looked rested. Always at her side, Tom kept her safe without restricting her. Sometimes, she'd reach out and touch his chest, arm, or shoulder to make sure he was real.

One overcast day at lunch, Tom brought up a sticky subject.

"What's your mission?" he asked, turning to glance at her before taking a bite of his sandwich.

"Don't know yet." Eden poured iced tea from a glass pitcher.

"I thought you were going after those guys."

"I am."

"You need a team."

"I'll have a team." Eden looked away.

"How about adding me?"

She stared at him. "You? Never?" She shook her head.

He bristled. "Not good enough?"

"Oh, no. Plenty good enough. Too…important…to me."

"Count me in," Mick said, taking a slug of unsweetened tea.

"I want to help, too," Tara piped up.

"You're all very sweet. But my I.S.'ll have a couple of men for me."

"You've got a couple of men right here."

"I'm not going to endanger your life, or Mick's, either."

Tom pushed away from the table and left the room. Eden came out of her seat, but Mick put his hand on her arm.

"Stay. I'll talk to him."

"I'm going for a walk on the beach," Eden announced, getting to her feet.

When Mick joined his buddy on the back deck, Eden doubled back. *They're not going to plan shit without me.* She circled the house, finding a spot just underneath them. She peeked through a space between the boards and saw the men's legs. They sat at the table there.

Eden dropped down under the deck and sat cross-legged in the sand, turning her ear toward the men. She could hear every word perfectly.

"I don't like it, Mick. She's not prepared for this."

"You don't know that. And you don't know who her team is going to be, either."

"She's not like other women. Not for me. Standing by, helpless, knowing she's going back there…It makes me crazy."

Eden's eyes watered. For a split second, guilt at her eavesdropping entered her heart. But a warm feeling of love pushed it away. *How did I get so lucky to find you, Davis?*

"I get it. But I doubt there's anything you can do."

"But I don't have to like it."

"No, you don't."

"I've been thinking. Someone might be leaking her location. Not sure I trust her I.S. I'm going to call Staff Sergeant Martin and get some background on that asshole."

Good idea! Eden smiled and nodded from her secret place, careful to keep silent. *He's got the ears of a cat.*

"She'll have to tell you who he is first, won't she?"

"Yeah. I've got my ways." Tom snickered.

Mick laughed.

Eden pushed out her lower lip and furrowed her brow. *Got his ways! Why that sneaky bastard. I'm onto you.*

"When my leave is over, I don't know where I'm going to be. Can I give him your contact info? Would you gather the data for me? Call me if you see a problem. If the guy's clean, fine. If not, I need to know."

"What about the secretary?"

"Might as well throw her in the mix. She's pretty close to Eden, too."

"You're not going to tell her you're doing this?"

"The fewer people who know, the less chance for a slip-up. Besides, you know Eden. She'd have my head if she knew I was doing this."

Damn straight, I would.

"You got that. Especially behind her back."

They both laughed.

Who's got the last laugh, eh? She smiled.

"Deal?"

"Deal. Have your man send the intel to me."

"I'll be in touch. We've got to keep this under the radar. Don't want anyone to know what we're doing."

"How about a code name?" Mick suggested.

"Okay. Code name Saving Grace."

"Works for me. Now, you gotta go back in there and play nice."

"I know. But I don't have to like it," Tom repeated.

Panic seized Eden. She scrambled quietly out from under the deck and scurried around to the front door. She joined Tara in the kitchen, grabbing a towel and picking up a wet dish.

"Find any shells?" her friend asked.

"Nope." She was out of breath, but trying to steady it.

The two men returned to the kitchen where the women were putting food away.

"It's cleared up outside. Want to go for a walk? Shopping?" Tom asked Eden.

"Sure. As long as the subject of my mission is closed."

"It is, honey. Let's go." He took her hand, and they headed for the beach.

"Only a couple of days left. No fighting. Okay?"

"Got it. Let me buy you something as a souvenir," Tom said, swinging their joined hands.

"What did you have in mind?" *Yeah, the subject of my mission is closed? I don't think so.*

"Hmm… Maybe a dress, or one of those handmade shawls we saw…or an engagement ring?"

Eden stopped. "What did you say?"

"A dress or a shawl."

"I thought that's what you said."

"Works for me."

She moved closer, snaking her arm around his waist. Tom rested his on her shoulder.

"Have I told you lately that I love you?" she asked, quietly.

"Uh, nope. Don't think so."

"Well, I do."

"Me, too, beautiful." They walked in silence along the sand, carrying their shoes and listening to the waves.

* * * *

Tom made reservations at the Amalie Inn, the best restaurant on the Island, for their last dinner before parting. They agreed to keep it only the two of them. Mick and Tara ate at home.

Eden donned the dress Tom had bought her. It was of a soft and gently draping cotton. The print was colorful, with turquoise, green, and gold swirling throughout. The halter neck left her shoulders bare. The back was cut low, so she wore no bra. The dress clung a bit, outlining her breasts and hips. Native earrings, her favorite perfume, flowing hair caressing her back, and subtle make-up finished off the look.

When she joined him in the living room, he was speechless.

"What's the matter, Davis?"

"You look…I can't describe it."

"Something showing?" Eden looked down her front and back, but didn't find anything out of place.

"I've never seen a woman…You're beyond beautiful."

She smiled at him. He looked so handsome in his uniform that she wanted to jump his bones. *Dinner first.* Tom offered his arm, and Eden wound hers through, resting her hand on his forearm.

Once seated in the restaurant, they were quiet. Eden closed her eyes, enjoying the cool, evening breeze as she sipped her piña colada. She tilted her chin up and found a star. *I wish Davis and I could stay like this forever.* A sudden sadness swept into her heart. Her eyes filled, and she looked away.

Tom frowned. He lifted her face to him. "What's wrong?"

"Trying not to think. It's our last night. I want to be happy. It's hard."

He gave a rueful smile. "Yeah, I know."

"We may never be together again. One of us may get killed. Or meet someone else and fall in love."

Tom shook his head. "I'll never find anyone else like you."

"You never know."

"I get it. We both know that in this business, that's the chance you take. Hell, people get hit by buses, too. Life is, well, no guarantees."

"I hate that. We make the odds against us higher."

"Maybe. But it's what we do."

"Right now, I wish I was a school teacher."

Tom chuckled. "Then, you wouldn't be here, with me."

"I'd probably be getting it on with the principal…no, wait, the school superintendent."

He laughed. "Sounds about right."

She smacked him in the arm.

"Eden, wait. Seriously. If we get through this…" He hesitated.

She sat still, staring at him.

He took a deep breath. "If we get through this…"

"Yeah? You said that."

He took her hand. "Would you… I mean…would you consider… I mean…could we be together, like all the time?"

"A commitment?"

"Yeah."

"Didn't I say no commitments?"

"So?"

It was her turn to laugh.

"This isn't a hook-up, Eden. It's more. Much more. I don't want to say goodbye." He held her fingers to his lips.

"Neither do I. I don't know how you did it, but I can't say 'no'."

"So, we're committed?"

She nodded.

"Maybe sort of…engaged?"

She took a sip of her drink and choked. "Engaged?"

"Yeah. That's sort of committed."

"You have to propose to be engaged."

He started to rise up from his seat.

She pushed down on his arm. "Don't. Don't do that. Commitment is one thing. But that...that..."

He ignored her and pushed to his feet. Tom reached into his pants pocket and bent down on one knee.

Eden covered her face with her hands. "I'm not seeing this. You're not doing this."

He knelt before her, a diamond ring in his hand. "Eden. Will you marry me?"

She peeked out, and her eyes grew wide. "Oh, my God. Didn't I tell you not to do that?"

"And I didn't listen. Will you?"

A tear slipped down her cheek. She swiped it away with the back of her hand.

"Look at me. Tell me you don't love me," he said.

"I can't. I can't lie to you."

"So, let's get married."

"Why?"

"Because we love each other and want to be together. Maybe have kids?"

Her heart pounded in her chest. She knew she couldn't live without him. Taking his face in her hands, she whispered, "Yes. No. Wait."

"Did you say 'yes'?" He cocked his head.

She nodded. "What if we agree to get married when we get back?"

"You mean if we survive?" he asked.

"Right. I want something to think about, to shoot for. Something to come back to," she said.

"And if we're engaged, you'll have it."

Tom went to slide the ring on her finger. She stopped him.

"The ring. I want to come back for the ring. Besides, it's too dangerous to wear it. Someone'll know you're in my life. They'll come after you. We need to keep it a secret."

"I agree. But for tonight, wear it."

"It's beautiful." She beamed at him, slipping it on. Happiness swelled her heart.

"Now, we both have something to come home to." He leaned over and kissed her.

Eden relaxed. *I want to remember this forever.*

"You'll be Mrs. Davis."

"What?"

"Mrs. Davis."

She burst out laughing. "I guess I'll have to call you Tom, then, won't I?"

"Yep."

"It's a helluva long way to go to get me to call you by your first name."

"But well worth it."

"Your dinner, sir?" The waiter arrived with two plates of Mahi Mahi. Eden and Tom sat back and stared at each other while the food was laid out before them. When they returned to the house, they could barely get the door to their room closed before ripping each other's clothes off.

"Take it easy on the uniform," Tom whispered.

She giggled. When she was naked, she leaped onto the bed.

Tom eased down quietly. "I'm going to make love to you all night long. Don't want you to forget me."

"I'll never forget you. All night works for me. Tomorrow I can sleep on the plane."

"Where you headed?" He began kissing her neck.

"Washington to meet my team then on to Beirut."

"Beirut?"

"Lion's gotta go where the prey is."

"Okay, lioness. But we're here, now." He cupped her breast and lowered his head.

"You mean you don't want to think about it?" she whispered, running her fingers through his chest hair.

"Nope."

"Figured."

"Let's go somewhere else," he said.

"How about Nirvana?" she asked, as she began to kiss her way down his body.

"Sounds like a plan." He buried his hands in her golden locks.

Chapter Nine

Restless, Eden rolled over for the millionth time. She inched closer to a sleeping Tom, cuddling into his back. She glanced at the clock and sighed. *Five. Not going back to sleep.* She slid quietly out of bed and slipped on her robe.

In the kitchen, she put up a pot of coffee. After filling a mug, she stole silently through the sliding glass doors onto the deck. She placed her drink on the railing and watched the sun rise. Her mind raced at a hundred miles an hour. *How many will be on my team? Guys or guys and girls? Will I have to go back to that awful house? Do I have to be inside that place? Can I do it and keep my cool? Will Davis wait for me? Will I survive or will they be waiting for me?*

She bit her lip, and her brows knitted as she stared at the red sun rising from the horizon. A hand on her shoulder made her jump. She sloshed coffee onto the floor.

"Davis, you gave me a heart attack."

"Sorry, beautiful. Didn't mean to." He tugged her into his embrace.

"Not much time," she muttered.

"When does your plane leave?"

"Nine."

"Nope. Not much."

She spread her legs a bit to ease the slight soreness there, left over from non-stop lovemaking. The twinge made her smile at the memory. She'd never had a lover like Tom. Even Jerry couldn't keep up.

The lieutenant colonel glanced down. "Something bothering you?"

"A little sore. It's nothing."

"I'm sorry. I'd never hurt you." He hugged her to his chest.

"I know. I didn't want to stop." She giggled.

"Guess I got carried away. You do that to me."

"Same here."

They stood together until the sound of the sliding door caught their attention. Mick and Tara joined them.

"It's almost seven," Mick said before bringing his cup to his lips.

Eden pulled away from Tom. "Time to get dressed."

Half an hour later in the taxi, Eden pulled the ring from her finger. She dropped it in the palm of Tom's hand and closed his fingers around it. "That had better be waiting for me when I get back."

"It will."

She turned full eyes to him. "Not gonna cry."

He kissed her. "Come 'ere, beautiful," he said, tucking her into his shoulder. Eden relaxed against him, breathing deeply, fixing his scent in her brain.

At the entrance for departures at the airport, the cab stopped, Tom paid the driver, and took her suitcase inside. They held hands until the security line separated them.

"I'm coming back," Eden said.

"You'd better. Or I'll come and find you."

"You will?"

"Damn right, I will. You're not getting away from me that easy."

"Same goes for you."

"Yeah?"

"Yeah. And that..." She pointed to his closed fist. "Had better be waiting for me," she repeated.

"You can count on it."

"I do. Be safe, Davis."

"Still with Davis?"

She laughed. "Be safe, Tom, my love."

"That's better."

She waved at him until she went through the door. The walk to the aircraft took only a few seconds, but when she turned, the door was closed, and he wasn't visible. Eden sighed as she climbed the stairs. Hugging the wall, she peered out the tiny window, searching for a glimpse of her lover.

The plane had begun to move before she spotted him, standing on the sidewalk in front of the building, waving. She blew a kiss then pulled out a tissue to blot her eyes. *Will I ever see you again? Feel your touch? Please, God, I hope so.*

The small jet taxied down the short runway, picking up speed quickly. She was airborne before she even noticed. Settling back in her seat, Eden closed her eyes. *I have so many memories.* She ran through the images of them in her mind. It was like watching her own personal documentary.

Eden took a taxi to the Jefferson Smith hotel, down the block from the CIA offices. A nondescript place, the Agency held several rooms there on contract. She wasn't sure how secure they were, but they were convenient. She figured she wouldn't be there long. After rinsing out some underwear in the sink, she changed to winter clothes and headed to the office to meet her team.

Lynn Downing greeted her with a hug. The woman kept her figure at forty-seven, though her hair was going a bit gray. Red lipstick outlined her broad smile. "You're looking wonderful for a woman who was shot at two weeks ago."

"I recuperate well," Eden said. She'd decided not to tell anyone about Tom. Besides, her private life was her own business.

"He's waiting to see you."

Eden nodded, knocked, and then opened the door to her boss' office. He stood up when she entered.

Sumner Smith was a good-looking man. In his late forties, he had dark hair with a touch of gray at the temples. He kept a trim body by working out in the gym at the Agency during lunch. Light brown eyes twinkled at her as a smile crinkled his forehead. He wore a charcoal gray suit, white shirt, and magenta tie. The outfit on his tall frame looked powerful, giving him authority along with a bit of sexiness.

"Sumner." Eden extended her hand.

He took it in his. "Eden. How nice to see you. And in one piece."

"You know me. Can't hit a moving target."

He chuckled. "How was your R and R?"

"Fine. When do I meet my team?" The warmth in his eyes made her uneasy. She'd had a short-lived relationship with him and always wondered if he'd been serious about her. When she had been unattached, she'd considered staying with him and had decided against it because of the possible danger to them both. He had bowed to her wishes, but seemed unhappy about her decision. A rueful smile crossed her lips when she realized she had that now with Tom anyway.

"Are you sure you want to do this?"

"Are we on this merry-go-round again? I thought it was settled. Yes, I want to do this, and no, you can't stop me."

"Damn dangerous. And unnecessary."

"You may think living your life looking over your shoulder is fine, but I don't. I want to live like everyone else."

"Then what are you doing at the Agency?" He laughed.

"That's not funny."

"I know. I know. Why all of a sudden? You seemed content to let things lie a month ago."

"That was then, and this is now. Came to my senses." *Sure as hell not telling you about Tom.*

His gaze examined her. His mouth was grim, his eyes suspicious.

Never easy to fool Sumner. She shifted in her chair, wishing he'd turn his attention somewhere else.

"Is there a special man in the picture?"

"Was. No longer. Easy come, easy go."

Sumner relaxed. He sat back in his chair and smiled at her. "Someday you'll settle down."

"Yeah. Someday. In the meantime, there are a few assassins I need to clean out of my life. Where's my team?"

"I got you two men. Blake and Sherman. They'll meet you at the Capital Café on 14th and Pennsylvania. You know the drill."

"Yeah. Meet upstairs. Thanks, Sumner." She pushed to her feet.

"You're very valuable to us, Eden. Professionally…and I've gotten used to having you around."

"Thanks. I've gotten used to having me around, too."

Sumner nodded. "New hair color isn't bad. You should blend in well."

"Thanks." She shook his hand and left.

Lynn led her into a supply section and handed her a gun and ammunition. In a sealed plastic bag was her new identity. Eden opened the bag. Everything was there, just needed a photo.

"Elsa Greer? Couldn't you come up with something sexier?" She handed the packet back.

"We used that for your grandmother. Thought it might bring you luck."

"For Gram, huh? Yeah. That makes it lucky."

"You'll take it and like it. Here. Let me get a new pic."

Eden stepped in front of the camera, and Lynn took the shot.

"Pick it up tomorrow before you leave."

"Will do." Eden stuffed the bag into her purse along with the weapon and ammo.

"Good luck, sweetheart," Lynn said, giving her a hug.

"Thanks." Eden returned the embrace.

"Anything to confess before you leave?" Lynn arched an eyebrow.

"Not a thing. Life has been very quiet."

"Where were you?"

"Relaxing on the beach."

"Alone?"

Eden stuck out her lower lip. "Unfortunately."

"That's too bad. An attractive woman like you. By the way, I hope you intend to go back to blonde when this mission is over."

Eden bristled a little, but hid it well. "We'll see. Might go darker. You never know."

Lynn opened the door, and Eden headed for the elevator. Once outside, she walked to 14th Street. *Two guys in my team? Pretty small. They'd better be good.* She shivered a second, not sure if it was from the cold or the impending peril she was about to encounter.

Lights were on at the Capital Café. Small bells sounded when she opened the door. She found a tiny, empty table in the back corner and ordered chai tea and a croissant. Munching quietly, she looked over the patrons. One older woman. Two men, not sitting together. *Could be them.* At the sound of the bells, Eden turned to see a medium-sized man with a dark beard and mustache enter the little shop, glance at her, and then take a seat near the entrance.

She finished her food then rose up, disappearing through the arch that said "restrooms" on a wood plaque above. She opened the door that said "closet" and another one at the back. She climbed a steep spiral staircase as quietly as she could. At the top, she punched in a numeric code, and the door clicked open.

Inside was a coffee machine and a hot water dispenser, as well as all the fixings for coffee and tea. In the corner stood a small refrigerator. There was no window, and the walls were metal.

Eden sat at the round table in the center of the room. Restless, she arose and poured a cup of coffee. She paced until she heard the door click.

A tall man, at least six foot one with short, sandy blond hair came through it. He nodded once at Eden and took off his stocking cap. "Blake."

"Elsa Greer." They shook hands.

The man got himself a cup of coffee too and slumped down in a chair, waiting for the third member of the team. He didn't have long to wait. Before he drank half his cup, the door opened again. The medium-sized man Eden had seen in the café entered. They all shook hands, and Sherman, the new guy, got coffee as well.

"Plane for Germany leaves in two days. Have to wait for Greer's I.D.," Blake said.

"Then Ankara. We pick up weapons there and drive to Beirut," Sherman added.

"What's the set up there?"

"The bastard's younger brother moved into the house after you killed them all. He took over the wife and mistress. There are a couple of servants who come and go, but we haven't spotted any regulars living there except two bodyguards," Blake explained.

"Then where are the assassins?" Eden wondered.

"How many were there in New York?" Sherman asked.

"Four. Three are dead, one in jail," Eden replied.

"We need to get in there." Blake rubbed his chin.

Eden headed for the coffeemaker. "Any ideas?"

"Yep. Sumner suggested you go in as a maid. Are you up to it?" Blake asked.

She nodded. "Gotta get this finished. I need my life back."

"First, a few changes." Sherman got up and went to the cabinet. He rifled through some boxes before pulling out a scissors. He walked over to Eden and put his hand on her shoulders. "Relax. It's only hair." Before she could answer, he'd cut off a hank of her long locks.

She jumped then murmured her assent. Sherman moved around her, chopping off her tresses until they hung down, lank, just below her ears.

She pulled out her compact and gasped. Tears clouded her eyes for a moment until she blinked them back. *Davis loves my hair. Stop. Can't think about him now. He could be gone forever.* "Thanks, Sherman."

"Something else." He pulled out a nail clipper and led her over to the table, where he cut off each long fingernail, trimming down until they were as short as possible.

She grunted with each cut of the first three nails then composed herself. Remembering how Tom loved the way she scratched his back with her long claws, sadness swept through her heart for a moment.

"There. You don't resemble the woman you were before."

Again, she glanced in the compact mirror. "Yep. I can pass for a maid."

"If you keep those luscious blue eyes cast down, you'll pass," Blake put in.

She gave him a lopsided grin. "I'll do what I gotta do."

Sherman pulled sandwiches from the refrigerator while Eden poured coffee. When they sat down, she continued to question.

"So, what's the plan?"

"Car bombings are still taking place. We need to get those guys into a car then blow it up." Blake took a bite of his food.

"How are we going to do that?" Sherman inquired.

"Kill 'em first. Then haul their asses down, after dark," Blake replied.

"Blow the car just after daybreak?" Eden asked.

"Girl's got brains. Yeah. That's the plan." Blake stuffed a small piece of ham in his mouth.

"What about the brother?" Eden finished her roast beef.

"We take him out when the car blows."

"Synchronize?" Sherman asked.

"Yeah. No one'll know or pay attention to the house once the bomb goes off."

"Then, we split immediately. Job done." Blake sat back and polished off his coffee.

Sherman looked at Eden. "What if someone recognizes you?" He took the last bite of his ham and cheese.

"No one's left from before."

"But the guys in New York knew you. Where to find you," Sherman continued.

"I know. Don't worry about it. That's my problem. Gotta handle this first."

"But if they recognize you, then we all go down."

"Look, I told you." She pushed to her feet and began to pace. "I killed them all at the house, and the one left alive in New York is in jail. No one at that house is going to recognize me."

Blake went to a dresser and opened a drawer. "In here, Elsa. Clothes. Pick out a couple of dresses." Then, he went to the closet and fished out a small valise. "This is your new suitcase. And wash that makeup off your face."

Eden plucked a few garments in her size from the drawer and packed them. She scrubbed her face until it hurt and removed her earrings. Gazing in the mirror, her heart ached. *Would Davis give this chick the time of day? Probably not.* She sighed.

"This isn't a fucking beauty contest, Greer. Stop mooning and get your stuff. Our plane leaves in two days." Blake threw his coffee cup in the trash and left.

Sherman stood and offered his hand. Eden took it.

"I've heard about you. Looking forward to working together," he said.

"Me, too." She managed a smile.

He went out the door and down the stairs. Eden checked her watch. When fifteen minutes had passed, she left.

Eden had lived in Washington, so she had no desire to do any sightseeing during the two days she waited for her new identity. Instead, she lay in bed, reading, eating, and watching television. The morning they were due to leave, a package arrived. The bellman delivered it to her room.

She ripped it open to find her new passport, driver's license, and a wallet stuffed with three-hundred thousand Lebanese Pounds, about two hundred U.S. dollars. She threw underwear, toothbrush, toothpaste, a brush, and socks into the valise along with the clothes Blake had given her. She returned her cell phone, earrings, and watch back to her duffle bag along with her real identification.

She donned a lighter weight coat because winter in Lebanon only got as low as fifty degrees most days.

After stuffing her down jacket in her luggage, she brought everything down to the private room in the back of the hotel. She put the combination of 717 into the lock and stowed her gear in the locker. *Hope I live to come get this stuff.*

With her last American dollars in her pocket, Eden caught a cab to the airport. Sitting back against the cushioned seat, she thought about her life. On the brink of either snuffing out the problem or getting snuffed herself, her nerves were on high alert. The desire to flee into a dark crevice of the Earth and hide grew strong in her belly. *To hide out with Davis for the rest of my life.*

Her smile faded when she realized Davis would never spend his life hiding. He'd be brave. Stand up for himself. Do the right thing. She sighed. *If I want to survive, I have to stop thinking about Tom. Completely. If I'm not totally focused, I'll make a mistake and die. I miss him so much already. Damn. he got under my skin fast. Okay. I'll think about him all the way to the plane, but once I get on...that's it. No more until the mission is over.*

As the vehicle whizzed past the Jefferson Memorial, Eden allowed her mind to wander. Of course, it ended up in bed with Tom. She smiled as she remembered their heated last night together. She'd never been with such an attentive, passionate lover. He never took his hands, or mouth, off her body.

She shivered at the memory of his touch and the heat from his skin on hers. One minute he was gentle, the next alpha, demanding, taking her. She loved it, loved him, and surrendered gleefully. She chuckled. Giving in to a man's desires hadn't been on her agenda in a long time. With Tom it was different, everything was different.

The cab pulled onto the turnoff for the airport. The drab government buildings and the grayness of the clouds overhead did nothing to lighten her mood or distract her from her thoughts. Row after row of the uniform structures blended in with the long runways, never masking their purpose, nor taking her mind off Tom or the island.

The taxi arrived too soon. Eden wasn't finished replaying their amorous evening. When her feet hit the ground, the memory of Lieutenant Colonel Tom Davis was locked away, behind a sealed door in her mind. She became Elsa Greer. Her mouth drooped at the corners, and her eyes scoured the ground, only peeking up to keep from running into people and walls. She'd be playing a role soon. Might as well start now.

The hangar's drab grayness added to the weight of the intensity of her mission. The lack of decorations, logos, or advertisements amplified the seriousness of the military airport, almost causing her to have second thoughts. The men and women in uniform preparing the flight for take-off moved all around Eden, ignoring the fact that she was there. *All the better to be invisible and unnoticed.*

She found her way to the right office. Blake and Sherman were there already, sitting at a round table. A stranger stood, holding a large envelope, talking to them.

"Greer," Eden said, extending her hand to the man in front of her.

He held hers in a firm grip. "Smith."

She laughed. "That's original."

"I've got the house plans and car keys. Also instructions on how to find where you're staying. Greer, you're going as Blake's wife and Sherman's sister." Smith shoved a thin, gold band on the fourth finger of her left hand. Eden flashed back for a moment to the same motion by Tom, but with a beautiful diamond ring. She recalled how it glittered in the light, unlike this dull one, shamefully claiming her.

"You'll fly to Germany. Then Jerusalem. A car is waiting in the parking lot there. You'll find a map in the glove compartment. License plate is on the keys in here." He rattled a manila envelope. "Three disposable cells in here, too. You each have a code. It's three numbers. Same as your locker combination at the hotel. Anyone have a problem with that?"

Everyone shook his or her head.

"Good. Questions?"

"When the mission is complete, how do we get out?"

"Drive back to Jerusalem. Contact Sumner. There will be a plane waiting for you. You'll fly back to Germany as soon as you're able."

"What do you mean 'able'?" Sherman asked.

"Presuming you have no injuries."

"Damn right, we'll have no injuries," Blake muttered.

Smith stood up. "Everything clear?"

The trio nodded.

"Good luck." Smith handed the envelope to Eden. She tucked it under her arm and boarded the plane with her team. Once they were in the air, she ripped it open and handed out the phones. Sherman took the directions to their apartment, Blake swiped the car keys, and Eden opened the house plans.

Simply looking at the drawing sent a spike of fear up her spine. *You're safe. Nothing is going to happen to you. You've got backup.* She peeked at her team and wondered how good they were with guns and if they could fight.

Sherman looked up. His brown eyes connected with hers. "Don't worry, Elsa. You'll be okay. We've got you."

"Yeah," Blake added, pulling his gaze from the window. "We won't let them get you. This time, we have the upper hand."

Eden managed a grim smile. "I hope so. I sure as hell hope so."

The flight was uneventful. Eden studied the blueprints over and over again because something seemed to be wrong. She shrugged. *Guess I won't know until I get there.* After two hours, she folded the papers up and stuffed them in her suitcase. She leaned back in her chair and closed her eyes.

A vision of Tom on the beach appeared in her head. She shook it slightly, forcing the image away, willing herself to become Elsa Greer, wife to Blake and sister to Sherman. Once the picture was gone, sleep followed.

Slowly opening her eyes to a pitch-black room, she turned to him and ran her finger over his jaw. "Love you," she murmured, snuggling up to him. He pulled the blankets up higher, covering their naked bodies. When they heard a noise in the hall, Jerry placed his finger on his lips. He sat up as the door flew open and five masked men burst into the room.

The first one raised the AK-47 and pulled the trigger, striking Jerry in the forehead. He went down. Brain matter splattered on Eden's arm. The second one came up to her, pointing the gun in her face and speaking to the others in Arabic. One of them grabbed her clothes from the chair and threw them at her. Her fingers trembled violently as she tried to get dressed. Jerry lay dead beside her on the bed, his lifeless eyes open and staring. Tears clouded her eyes as fear shot through her body.

Eden jolted awake. Looking around, she regained her bearings. She was on her way to get rid of the men who had murdered Jerry and were trying to kill her.

A grim smile stretched her lips. "I'm avenging Jerry and taking my life back." She sat up and looked out the window. Maybe she'd have to learn to live with the nightmares, but the possibility of happiness with Tom waited for her on the other side.

Chapter Ten

Tom tried to be sociable in St. Thomas, but after Eden left he found it hard to concentrate. His thoughts kept returning to her. Visions of her soft body under his, or the deep sound of her laughter, haunted him. Worry about her safety nagged at him, souring his mood, turning him sullen and quiet. *Damn her. Why'd I have to fall for her? I don't need this. I've got my own mission to worry about.*

But he couldn't escape. His heart was restless. He needed Eden in a way he'd never thought he'd need a woman. And it was her, and only her, who would do. Mick and Tara tried to include him in their plans, but he stood apart. Being with them helped on one level, but hurt on another. He was the third wheel, a man incomplete.

Only two more days. Tom got his clothes ready and packed early. He took one more shopping trip, buying some jewelry and a couple of dresses he thought would be beautiful on his girl. He needed to do that—think of her as his, as coming back, their missions simply small interruptions in the life they would begin together soon.

The night before he left, he had one more conversation with Mick about intel. This time, he included Tara.

"How'd you worm those names out of Eden?" Mick asked.

"Honestly? It was easier than I thought," Tom said. "I'm still wondering how those jackasses found her. Who ratted her out?"

"Had to be someone on the inside," Mick said, sipping a piña colada.

"But she's only talked about two people," Tara added.

"I know. And she trusts them. Undercover agents like Eden aren't known to everyone. They have to protect them. The fewer people who know who she is, the safer she'll be," Tom explained.

"So, it's gotta be one of those two, right?" Mick asked.

"Seems to be."

"You think the intel will tell us who it is?"

"I hope so. Then, we need to warn Eden."

"How are you going to do that?" Tara inquired.

Tom's mouth formed a grim line. "That's a good question, Tara. I don't know."

"You might have to wait until she comes back."

"I might, if that's not too late. What's to keep this...this mole from trying to have her killed on her mission? It would be convenient, easy to explain."

Mick put his hand on Tom's arm. "Don't think about that. When the intel comes in, I'll call you. Right away. But for now, we have to wait."

"That's always the hardest part."

"Another drink, guys?" Tara pushed to her feet.

"Make a pitcher."

"Aye, aye," she said, saluting.

Mick chuckled. "She likes to do that. Makes me laugh every time."

"You're lucky, Mick. Since you met Tara, I've been hoping to find one like her."

"Now, you've got Eden."

"Do I? If she survives."

"You getting married?" Mick asked.

Tom blushed and dropped his gaze. "I proposed the night before she left."

"Well, son of a bitch. Why didn't you say so? She accept?"

Tom nodded. He pulled the ring out of his pocket and stared at it. "Yep."

"We could've been celebrating. Why didn't you say something?"

"Didn't want to jinx her return. She put it on hold until she gets back."

Mick glanced at the ring. "That's why you still have that?"

"Yep."

Tara returned with a pitcher of piña coladas. She spied the ring. "Gonna propose?" Her eyebrows shot up.

"You're two steps behind. He already did. They're engaged," Mick said, pulling her into his lap.

"Why do you have the ring?" Tara asked. Tom explained while she refilled their glasses.

"Fantastic. Let's have a toast." She lifted her drink.

"To Eden's safe return," Tom said, a slight quaver in his voice unmistakable.

Tom retired early, though he wasn't tired. He lay in the bed he'd shared with Eden, fingers laced behind his head, staring out the window at the moon. A million thoughts ran scattered through his mind. He pictured her by his side in a house with a white picket fence and two small children on the swings in the backyard.

"Fat chance," he mumbled to himself. *Eden's not a homebody type, is she?* He shook his head. *Always looking for adventure? Maybe. Maybe ready to settle down.* He wondered if the quiet life was right for him, too. *Probably not.* But for the first time, the idea of a nice, stateside position where he'd be safe with her had tremendous appeal.

He rolled over and smoothed his hand over the sheet where she had lain. An intake of breath made him smile as he detected a faint whiff of her lilac perfume. No matter what happened, Tom knew he'd never be the same. If his wish came true and Eden returned in one piece, he'd be the happiest man alive. If she didn't, he realized he'd spend the rest of his life looking for another woman like her.

Gotta be positive. He shook off negative thoughts and turned his mind back to the good times with the love of his life. Closing his eyes, he pictured them on the beach, splashing and roughhousing in the surf, walking hand-in-hand along the shore, looking for shells. Then, his mind turned to randier thoughts.

He conjured up a picture of her, naked, waiting in bed for him. His fingertips tingled at the memory of her soft skin. She was the most exciting woman he'd ever made love to. And he'd had his share. None could compare to Eden. Her eagerness to make love and responsiveness to his touch revved him up, taking him to a place he'd never been before. She was an equal partner to him in every way. His heart's desire. His dream come true.

He fell asleep dreaming of being with her and slept peacefully through the night. The next morning, goodbyes were quick as Mick and Tara left him in the security line at the airport. Tom boarded the plane, uncertain where his future would take him, but convinced his heart was safe with the one-of-a-kind woman he called "beautiful."

After thirty-nine hours and three flight changes, Tom arrived. At the airport, he was met by Captain Fasper.

"Welcome back, sir. Hear you've been promoted."

"Yes. What've I missed?"

The Captain reviewed the events of the last two weeks while they drove to the camp.

"Sergeant Cromwell and Corporal Jenkins were killed by an IED when they were running a security sweep of a supply convoy. Lance Corporal Parkins lost both legs and is at Landstuhl recovering. Sergeant Stevens had a breakdown and is also at Landstuhl."

"Holy shit. Get me the addresses of the families. Keep me updated," Tom said.

"Command has given us an op for tonight—a 'snatch and grab' of Omar Youssef. This guy is well-connected and high in Al-Qaeda. He can give us intel on a list of safe havens, suppliers, and hideouts. Command wants details of any planned attacks."

"When and where?" Tom asked.

"In the Humvees at 0400. Your team is as follows—Sergeant Post, sniping, Staff Sergeant Platt, radio, Staff Sergeant Alexander, demolitions, and Staff Sergeant Martin, intel."

The command tent was as Tom had left it. He threw down his duffel and went to inspect his weapons, an M4 Carbine with suppressor and a MEUSOC 1911 pistol. He gathered five magazines of ammunition for each, a pair of AN/PVS-7B Night Vision Goggles, some rope, a Class I Type 3 survival/medical kit, and five grenades, two fragmentation and one smoke.

Exhaustion caught up with him. After inspecting his weapons and equipment, Tom sprawled out on his cot and slept. He dreamt of Eden, her lilac perfume, her fingertips on his skin, her kiss, and the sound of her voice.

His alarm went off at 0330 hours. He stretched then washed up. Staff Sergeant Platt lathered up his face at the next sink.

"You ready to get this guy, sir?" Platt asked, pulling out his razor.

"Absolutely, this asshole'll give us the intel to put a big hurt on Al-Qaeda."

The Humvees came to a stop a little over two miles from their target, a small house on the outskirts of the city. They covered the vehicles with desert camouflage nets, grabbed their gear, and started the trek to the house. It took a little over an hour to negotiate the flat, open terrain and unseen buildings.

Thump, thump was the only sound from Sergeant Post's sniper rifle, as two security men on the balcony slumped to the floor, dead. Davis and Platt took both sides of the door and donned the night vision goggles that would turn the blackness into day. Staff Sergeants Martin and Alexander took the back door and did the same.

At exactly 0500, both pairs of men burst through the doors. After a quick firing of Tom and Platt's weapons, two men to the left of Tom fell over dead before they could utter a sound to raise an alarm. Simultaneously, Martin dropped his two targets. Alexander signaled to Platt to head up the stairs. Platt and Davis started up slowly while Martin and Alexander covered their climb.

Once at the top, they met one more guard, which Platt dispatched quickly. Davis spotted the target, approached him, and sprayed Neothyl solution, a general anesthetic, to knock him out. Davis and Alexander picked up Youssef and threw him over Platt's shoulder to haul him back to the Humvee.

At full sprint, carrying the body back to the hummer took a half an hour. Once inside the vehicle, they cranked up and sped back to the Camp. Their next step would be to interrogate the man and obtain all of the vital intel that they could.

* * * *

Sherman put the key in the lock and jiggled it a couple of times before it turned. He opened the door and Eden drew her gun, approaching the living room of their apartment slowly. The space was tiny. The living room had a small table near the window and two folding chairs. The sofa was ratty. The room had a slightly rancid smell.

Blake went to the dirty windows and peeked out. "It stinks in here," he said, reaching for the latch.

Sherman stopped him with a hand. "Wait. Look out there before you open it."

Blake glanced outside. "Seems okay to me."

Eden inched her way into a room through a door at the back of the living room. It was dark, and there was no light switch.

"Sherman. Get in here with your flashlight." She didn't intend to put the gun down. Her fake brother entered and shone the beam. He pulled a cord in the middle of the ceiling and a bare light bulb threw light into the corners of the shabby bedroom. There was one double bed against one wall and a cot against another. A small dresser hugged the other wall and sported a lamp made from a basket topped by a grimy shade. Eden plunked her backpack down on the bed.

"Who do you want to bunk with?" Blake shot her a salacious grin.

"You can sleep with Sherman. I'll take the cot."

"Damn. Was hoping for those conjugal rights," Blake said, with a snicker, dumping his pack on the floor.

Sherman laughed. "You're gonna make me sleep with him? Damn." He shook his head.

Eden gave a tiny smile under wary eyes.

Blake announced, "Food. I'll go. Any preferences?"

"Something that doesn't make me sick."

"Got it." Blake left.

Eden locked the door behind him while Sherman checked cabinets in the miniscule kitchen. He opened a refrigerator that only came up to his waist.

"I doubt this thing works." He lit the stove with matches from his breast pocket.

Eden sank down on the sofa, got itchy, and moved to a folding chair. "Who knows what the hell is living in that thing. I'm not sitting there."

Blake returned with a bag. On the table, he unloaded a container of hummus, two dozen pieces of pita bread, bottled water, and a six pack of beer. Sherman pulled three glass plates down from a cupboard. He swiped over them with a damp paper towel. Then, he popped tops off three bottles of beer and handed them out. The trio studied the floor plans of the house as they ate.

"This stinkin' hole makes me want to finish this mission in about five minutes. Let's toss a couple of grenades in there and be done."

"We have to make it look like an Al-Qaeda. Car bombing. It's the only way," Eden said before stuffing a piece of bread, slathered with the spicy topping, into her mouth. Suddenly, she was hungry.

"She's right. We have orders."

"First, we scout out the house." Eden studied the blueprints. "Something doesn't seem right. It's not like I remember."

"Maybe they renovated," Blake said, his eyes full of mischief.

"I don't know about you, Blake, but this is serious to me." Her brows were knitted, her mouth compressed into a frown.

"Sorry." He patted Eden on the back.

She shrugged his hand off. "Keep your hands to yourself, or you'll wake up with no balls."

Blake scowled, but pulled away. "Trying to get along here."

"Do it without touching me." Eden replied.

"Chill, folks. Okay? We're in this together," Sherman said, raising his palms.

The others nodded and murmured their agreement.

"We're going in as service people tomorrow. Scope the place out," Sherman said.

"Okay. Tomorrow night, we'll finalize the plan. Day after, back in, finish off the assassins and blow them up," Blake said.

"You make it sound easy," Eden said.

"It is," Blake insisted.

"What about collateral damage?"

"Like?"

"Wife. Kids. We don't know who lives in that house."

"Okay, okay. Tomorrow night we'll figure out what to do with the bystanders."

"We can't leave any witnesses."

"Did you last time?"

"Yeah. One guy survived. That's why we're here," Eden said.

"Seems like we're good to go. Finish up. I'll wash the dishes tonight. Let's get some shut eye," Sherman suggested.

Eden stretched out, fully clothed, on the cot with a thin blanket folded over her. On assignment, she never knew when she'd have to spring in to action. So she never undressed when hitting the rack. She narrowed her eyes, watching the men get ready for bed. The back of her neck tingled. *Something's not right.* She didn't know exactly, but her instincts were never wrong. She placed her gun under her pillow, rolled over on her stomach, and curled her fingers around the cold, metal butt of the weapon. *No surprises. I'm done with surprises. For life.*

Her mind forgot Tom. Instead, memories of her nightmare in that house haunted Eden's sleep. She tossed on the tiny cot and woke up several times during the night. Her hands were shaking, her chest drenched in sweat. *Can I go in that house again?*

Fear spiked through her at the recollection...the smell, sickly sweet, of her captor's wife's cheap perfume. Horrifying memories flooded her mind like the banks of the Nile during rainy season. She couldn't shake the terrifying association with the dark red curtains, keeping her captivity a secret. The coldness of the tile floor under her feet or the hardness of it when she was smacked down. Every detail chilled her until her teeth chattered.

She arose and searched for a way to make a cup of tea.

Blake joined her. "Jumpy?"

She practically leapt out of her skin. "Might say that."

"With good reason. I couldn't sleep, either."

Eden sipped from her mug in silence.

"And when this is over?" Blake arched an eyebrow.

"I'll have a normal life again," she said.

"I'll drink to that." He toasted.

* * * *

An alarm clock woke the trio at seven. The sky was gray, but at least it wasn't cold. Eden smiled. *Sixty-eight degrees. Not St. Thomas, but not cold like New York.* The men dressed quietly, Eden changed her dress, then made tea. Together they finished the leftover hummus.

Blake took Eden's hand. "We're supposed to be married, Elsa."

"Okay, okay. Yeah." She stopped resisting. The warmth of his grip brought the unwelcome memory of Tom's fingers wrapped around hers. She gave her head a slight shake to chase the image away. *Focus, damn it. Gotta focus to stay alive.*

They crossed the street. Eden wrapped an ugly, brown and gray print scarf around her head and tied it under her chin. Within ten minutes, they were at the door of the house. *I have to blend in, be invisible.* Blake knocked.

A boy about age ten answered. Eden's eyes widened. *I'm not killing any kids.*

"Is your mother at home?" Blake asked, in Arabic.

The boy nodded and called over his shoulder, keeping the door only half open. A smartly-dressed woman with black hair and dark brown, suspicious eyes came over.

"We are here to work, missus. My wife, she cleans. I paint and my brother washes windows."

"I've been expecting you. Come in. Wipe your feet. Better, take off those dirty shoes."

She spoke well, as if she had been educated in an English-speaking school. *Will she be harder to fool? I hope not.* The trio slipped off their grimy footwear and padded into the house. Eden's gaze wandered around the first room.

"You can start cleaning here, in the living room. Did you bring your own supplies?"

Eden shook her head. *Better keep quiet as much as I can.*

The woman shrugged and made an annoyed sound. "Come with me then."

They walked into a large and well-appointed kitchen. *The house is well kept. Not much has changed since I was here.*

The woman pointed to the cabinet under the sink where the cleaning supplies were, turned her nose up, and issued an order. "I want the living room, den, and kitchen cleaned before you leave today. You can change the sheets and clean the bedrooms and bathrooms tomorrow." She left.

Eden gathered what she needed and returned to the living room. She dusted and swept, examining every crack and crevice for a secret door or panel.

She worked quickly so that she could get to the other rooms. The house was spacious. She had not been privy to all the private rooms and was anxious to search them. *Are they hiding the assassins back there?* Her curiosity got the best of her, and she wandered into a rear bedroom.

A voice stopped her. "What are you doing here?"

Eden gave her best blank stare. "Sorry. Lost?" The woman gave her shoulder a shove, sending Eden down the hall and back to the living room. Anger pooled in the agent's chest. *Calm down. You're going to win. Don't get riled.*

A deep breath and a shrug then Eden padded into the kitchen. Her eyes darted from wall to wall. The room seemed smaller than she remembered. She worked without speaking, but memorized every inch. They got a fifteen minute break for lunch. The woman tossed some stale bread and hard cheese on the table for them. They were hungry and devoured it quickly.

At the end of the day, Eden was exhausted and tense. They stopped for groceries and returned home, sequestering themselves in their grungy apartment. Sherman double locked the doors while Blake and Eden arranged the food. They had Baba Ghannouj and carrot and pea stew. Blake unpacked six brioches, three with dates and raisins and three with chocolate chips. Another two dozen rounds of pita were used like utensils, to scoop up the dip-like dishes.

After the pathetic lunch they'd had, the three were starving. They postponed talking about the house and the mission until they had filled their bellies.

Blake sat back and guzzled beer, giving forth a loud burp. "Excuse me." He eyed Eden.

"Shove it. I don't care." He made her skin crawl, and she couldn't wait to be back in the States again. Eden didn't trust either of her mission mates. She watched them with wary eyes.

"Anytime you want me to take him out, just say so," Sherman offered.

"Like you could," Blake sniffed before finishing his beer and letting go another loud belch.

"Cool it. Come on. We've got a job to do." Eden took a swig of her own drink.

"Okay, okay. We did our recon. No assassins. Can we go home now?"

"There was something wrong. Something missing. The house seemed too small. They must be hiding the assassins somewhere. Our intel tells us they're there."

"Okay. Another trip into that hell hole? Damn, I'm getting paint under my fingernails." Blake struck a pose then laughed.

"One more time. Otherwise, we report no assassins and go home," Sherman said, putting his empty bottle in the sink.

"Agreed."

Eden narrowed her eyes. "You can pick up stakes. But I've got to get them, or they'll get me."

Sherman patted her on the shoulder. "Don't worry. We'll get the bastards."

Blake nodded. Eden stretched out on her cot and opened a book, but she couldn't concentrate. *Something is strange about that house.* She closed her eyes and visions of her on the beach in St. Thomas with Tom floated through her head.

She smiled, giving in to the joy of remembering, and fell asleep.

Chapter Eleven

Tom paced in his office. He was expecting news on Eden's I.S. and the secretary, as well as new intel on known terrorist targets. This was his first mission as a lieutenant colonel, and the pressure to succeed was growing.

He filled his water pitcher, sharpened a few pencils, then sat down, and leaned back. Worry over Eden's mission and her safety rolled around in the back of his mind. He regretted not insisting upon being included. His team was strong. They'd be able to protect her from anything and take out the assassins who threatened her life. *Damn, bull-headed woman.*

He muttered to himself, wondering how he could have fallen for someone so stubborn so fast. Her independence was sexy, but not when her life was in danger.

"Colonel. Excuse me, sir," Staff Sergeant Martin interjected as he knocked. "I have some intel you'll be interested in," the tall, lanky man standing in the doorway said.

"What've you got?" Davis rose from his desk and took the papers from the Staff Sergeant.

"Hard to tell. Seems that..." Martin's face colored. He coughed and cleared his throat.

"Spit it out." Tom planted his fists on his hips.

"Seems that Ms. Wyatt had a relationship with the I.S., sir."

"Relationship?"

"Yeah. You know...the... uh...intimate kind?" Martin shifted his weight.

"You mean she was sleeping with her I.S.?"

"Appears to be so, sir."

"Hmm. Okay. Thanks. What else did you find out?"

"I am awaiting more details, sir. Would you like me to forward the intel to Sgt. Peterson when it comes in?"

"If I'm on a mission, yes. Otherwise, I'll take it here. Any trouble getting this?"

"Seems as if the couple did go to some lengths to cover it up, sir. But there is evidence—hotel room bills, restaurant bills, etcetera. Do you want the details?"

Tom's gut clenched. *Sometimes you'd rather not know.* "Ms. Wyatt's life may be at stake here, sergeant. We need all the intel we can get."

"Yes, sir. I'm on it." Martin saluted and returned to his tent.

Tom sank down in his desk chair and rested his forehead on his hand. *Eden. You might be in big trouble.*

An hour later, Martin returned.

"What now?" Tom's head pounded. *Eden, what else have you done?* He looked up and put his pen down. "More on Wyatt?"

"No, sir. This is different, sir."

"New intel?"

"Yes, sir. We have intel on a major terrorist mastermind, sir."

Tom rose from his desk and began to pace. "What have we got?"

"Location, sir. Seems as if he's in Iraq right now. Baghdad, to be exact," Martin produced a map and pointed to a circle drawn in pencil.

"Sit down. Let's go over this in detail." Tom laid the drawing out on his desk. Martin took a chair opposite.

"It's like this, sir," he began.

When Martin was finished, Davis said, "Get the team in here. They need to hear this, and we need to muster."

"Aye, sir."

Ten minutes later, Martin returned with Post, Platt, and Alexander.

"At ease," Davis said.

The men changed their stance and folded their hands behind their backs in the traditional parade rest position.

"Intel has given us another target. A big one. Anas El-Sherhi. They know where this guy will be and when. We have orders to return if possible, kill if necessary. This man cannot be allowed to escape at any cost. He has been the mastermind behind a few of the high level kidnappings, bombings, and assassinations." Davis spoke while he walked the length of the room.

"What's the plan?" Platt asked.

"Captain Franks and his men are studying the street and the building where he'll be. We'll spend the next two days training. We're going to learn the details of the structures, their layouts, and the neighborhood. I'll have the drawings and pictures on my desk when we reconvene. We must be prepared for anything, aiming for zero casualties. Chow at 0500 and meet at Command Tent 1 at 0600. Transport at 0700."

They acknowledged, and he dismissed them.

The men took turns on the computer, sending emails to their wives and girlfriends. Although they couldn't say what they were about to do or where they were going, each had code with his woman about the riskiness of the mission.

They needed to reconnect with their loved ones before marching into danger.

Davis walked by the computer station. Two men were on Skype.

"Yep, Daisy, I'm going to be washing the jeep in a few days," Platt said.

Davis saw Daisy's smile turn to a frown and a tear start to form as she understood the level of peril her man would encounter. Tom's mouth set in a grim line. The lives of these men were in his hands now. This needed to be done right with no casualties. He patted Platt on the shoulder as he passed.

Everybody's coming back in one piece. No more loss of life to terrorists on my watch.

* * * *

Beirut, Lebanon

Eden gathered the cleaning supplies and headed to the bedroom. She heard the doorbell ring before she had a chance to search. The woman of the house shouldered her aside, pushing her into the kitchen as a large bin was rolled into the space.

"Laundry. Do that room," she ordered, gesturing to a room down the hall as two men pushed the container into the master bedroom. Eden looked at it. A cloth draped over the top obstructed her view of the contents. It appeared to be full and heavy, as one man's arm muscles strained hard to move it.

Eden ducked into the other room. Placing her ear against the wall, she listened to the low sound of voices coming from next door. She fisted her hands in frustration at not being able to distinguish all the words spoken.

After fifteen minutes, she heard the squeak and roll of wheels. She peeked out and watched the men shove it out. The cloth sides fluttered a bit, as if the container was empty this time.

She went back to cleaning and feeling the walls for secret compartments. She didn't find anything. She jumped when the woman came into the room and ordered her back to her former task.

Eden tried not to smile, happy to be back in the master bedroom. It was empty. She was certain she heard voices, more than the two men and the woman, but there was no one else there. Eden was left alone and continued her search. Feeling along the walls, she kept one ear listening for footsteps while the other was keen on the muffled sounds.

She flattened her ear to the wall behind the bed. A soft murmur of voices almost sounded like a whistle of the wind. She focused her mind and held her breath. Her eyes flew open as she heard sounds, words, from more than one person. The words were not in English, and she cursed herself silently for not learning their language. *I don't need to know what they say, only that they are there. This is proof.*

At lunch, she signaled to her cohorts with her eyes, a smile, and the code word "red" that she had news. She turned to Blake.

"Can you buy me that red scarf I saw in the market?"

Blake's eye widened. "Maybe tomorrow. We'll see."

She cast her gaze to her food. Peeking up for a moment, she saw Sherman give a slight nod.

That night, they picked up dinner and locked themselves in their hideout. Eden was bursting to share.

"I found it."

"What?" Blake asked with his mouth full.

"There's a secret room behind a wall in the master bedroom."

"Fantastic. How do we get in there?" Sherman took a bite of pita bread.

"You go in there to clean the windows while Eden is vacuuming. That should give you enough cover if you make noise," Blake said.

They agreed on a plan and went to bed. Fear gripped Eden. *Can I trust Sherman and Blake? Sherman seems okay, but Blake is sneaky. I see him peeking at his phone when he thinks I'm not looking.*

Eden sent a text to Sumner.

Something's off. May need help fast. Advise.

He responded.

Trust your instincts. Code is "now."

She nodded, committed the S.O.S. word he gave her to memory, and closed her eyes. Again her mind saved her, remembering Tom's proposal and their romantic dinner. The memory of the delicious meal made her stomach growl. *I'm gonna overeat for a week if I get out of here.*

Then, her thoughts turned to their last night in bed together. Her blood pumped faster as she recalled the feel of his touch, his kiss, and him taking her with love and passion. A warmth suffused her body, lulling her to sleep.

The next morning, the three were admitted to the house. By now, the woman ignored them. This was what they had been hoping for, as now they'd have more freedom to explore. Sherman set up in the master bedroom. He and Eden went over every inch of the wall before they found an extra button on the light switch.

She stopped him from pushing it. "What if it's *the* room and we're suddenly standing here with our asses hanging out, facing two armed assassins?"

"Right, right."

They continued their search to make certain there were no other places that could spring a hidden door.

That night, they discovered a new wrinkle.

"What are we going to do with the family?" Eden asked before taking a bite of pita.

"The house has to be empty. We open the door, shoot the assassins, carry their bodies down to the car, and blow it up. Then, we're outta here." Blake sat back and took a swig of beer.

"She's right. What about the family? We're not authorized to kill them, too," Sherman said.

"A fire," Eden put in.

"What?"

"A fire. We'll have to start a fire. Then, we can get everyone out."

"But they'll be out in front. How can we get the bodies in the car?"

"Put the bodies in the backyard. Cover them with a tarp. Then put out the fire. Get the family back in. Return after dark to load the bodies. Boom. We leave."

"Where can we set a fire that won't get so big that we can't put it out?" Sherman asked.

"Good point. I don't know."

"The curtains. Those big, heavy things by the window in the living room?" Blake suggested.

"That should send everyone out fairly quickly."

"If we put the fire out before we get the assassins, it'll continue to smoke. So they won't come back in," Sherman said.

"How about a smoke grenade?" Blake scooped up hummus with pita.

"Perfect. Smoke grenade gets the family out of the house. Kill assassins and put them in the back. Then, set the fire."

"Fire department puts out the flames. When the family comes back inside, if the street is empty, we can load the bodies in the car. Sit 'em up, until dark," Sherman added.

"What if someone spots them?" Blake asked.

"That's the chance we have to take," Eden said. "And we'll have to get out immediately."

"Better start this right before we're supposed to finish for the day."

"Yeah. Like three thirty," Sherman agreed.

"We'll need a couple of days to get the stuff we need," Blake said.

"Crap. I hate going back there." Eden scowled.

Sherman patted her on the shoulder. "Only for a couple of days. Then, this will all be over."

"Two days? An eternity." She sighed.

"Don't worry. We've got this." Blake smiled.

They turned out the lights at ten.

Eden was restless. The plan was tight on time. Made her nervous. *I'm always nervous before a mission. Why should this be any different?* Lying on her side, she opened her eyes. After a minute to adjust to the pitch black of the room, she saw a tiny light. Blake was typing. His phone was mostly hidden under the covers, but she saw his arm move slightly. *Who is he texting? Why?*

Her pulse kicked up and adrenalin began to pump through her veins. *Don't know about Sherman, but Blake is definitely trouble. Now. Remember the word. Now.* She tried to lie still so as not to alert Blake that she was awake. It was difficult.

Breaking her rule again, she allowed herself to think about Tom. Envisioning their future together after this was over helped to calm her. Images of wedding dresses and a ceremony on the beach in St. Thomas occupied her mind until her exhausted body sought refuge in sleep.

* * * *

The next day, the trio searched Beirut for the supplies they needed. Smoke bombs were in the trunk of their car. They found a tarp, blow torch, and fire extinguishers after going to several stores.

"Fuck it. Time for a good meal," Blake said, steering them to the center of the city.

They entered the first fancy, expensive-looking restaurant they could find. After enduring the nasty stares at their clothes, they were seated at a table.

"Do you think we should make the CIA pay for this?" Sherman asked.

"Damn right. Who knows what will happen tomorrow," Eden said, placing her napkin in her lap.

"Kind of like our last supper, eh?" Blake's eyes twinkled, but Eden didn't laugh.

"I hope not. I've got places to go and people to see when I get out of this hell hole."

Blake raised his water glass. "Here's hoping you get your wish."

They ordered a fine meal and good wine. *I'd enjoy this more if I was sharing it with Davis rather than these two clowns.*

They walked back to their apartment and went over the plan one more time. Eden couldn't wait to get out of the shabby hole-in-the-wall. They packed their suitcases, keeping out only what they would need in the morning. They knew not to leave any trace of their presence in the place. They needed to be like ghosts, flying in to do their mission then disappearing as if they had never been there.

They stowed their backpacks and Eden's suitcase in the car, then parked it two blocks away from the house. Each loaded their weapon and stuffed as much ammo as they could in their pockets. The tarp was still in the packaging from the store. Eden held it under her dress, between her legs. She endured the suggestive jokes from the men and laughed with them. They needed something to relieve the tension.

They went about cleaning, painting, and washing windows. The family ignored them. Eden was so nervous she could barely choke down the hard, stale cheese and pita lunch left for them. Her gaze flicked back and forth between Sherman and Blake. When she went back to her task, she watched the hands of the clock on the wall inch along. *I could be dead in two hours. Blake and his "last supper" comment. Does he think I'm stupid?*

She patted her pocket to make sure she had her gun. At three thirty, they unwrapped the tarp and dropped the first smoke bomb. Eden screamed "Fire" and ran to gather the family. Sherman and Blake ushered everyone out quickly and locked the front door.

They dropped the second smoke bomb. The trio pulled out their HK45 combat tactical pistols with suppressors.

With no warning, Blake shot Sherman in the shoulder and the leg.

Eden's eyes widened. She whipped out her cell. She had already set it to Sumner and typed the word "now"—all she had to do was hit "send." Blake spun around and knocked the phone out of her hand. She leaped for it, but Blake closed his fist and smashed it into her face. Pain screamed in her head, but her fingers closed around the cell. She hit "send" before she crashed into a wall.

"Little thing like you should be easy to stop." Blake advanced on her, fists ready. Eden scrambled to her feet. She ducked him and ran out of the room. Sherman reached for his gun lying on the floor in front of him. Blake turned at the movement and shot him again before chasing after Eden. She hid in a closet, trying to hold her firearm steady with shaking hands.

"Come out, come out, wherever you are," Blake chanted, as he set off another bomb.

Smoke seeped under the door. Eden tried to refrain from coughing, but couldn't. Blake hacked in return before he whipped it open. Eden fired and nicked his side. He swore and grabbed her by the collar of her dress with one hand, throwing her into the wall. Her gun discharged and went flying.

Blake cursed again, feeling his side as Eden fought back the pain. He eyed her with fury. "You fucking bitch. You were the target, you know. All along."

"So, you're not going to bother with the assassins?"

"Hell no. Who cares about them? You're the one going under the tarp and in the car. Then, it's boom, baby. Bye, bye," he said, staring at her with cold eyes and an evil grin plastered across his face.

Fear sliced through Eden's body. The adrenaline rush pushed the pain out of her brain. Survival mode kicked in. She lunged for her gun, but Blake crushed her fingers under his foot. She bent in the middle and kicked the back of his knee, bringing him down. Rubbing her hand, she leapt to her feet and took off.

The smoke was clearing in the living room. Sherman was lying on the floor, not moving. She reached down with her good hand, and touched his neck, seeking a pulse. There was none. He was dead. Eden grabbed the blowtorch. Her fingers trembled so badly she could hardly light it, but she managed and pushed it toward the heavy draperies. The flames licked the fabric, which caught almost immediately. She lit everything she could find on fire.

"What the fuck are you doing?" Blake asked, creeping into the room.

"Stay away. I'll burn your sorry ass to the ground." Eden waved the torch at him.

He raised his gun and fired, nicking her arm. She ran past, scorching him, setting his clothes aflame as she scampered by, leaving the living room engulfed. She retrieved her pistol and headed for the master bedroom. She had her mission.

Eden heard banging on the wall. She fired into the plaster, saving three rounds for Blake. Flattening herself against it and ignoring the screaming pain from her busted hand and swelling face, she aimed at the door. With broken fingers, Eden couldn't steady the weapon. She held it with her good hand and muttered a quick prayer.

Blake rushed into the room, looking around. She squeezed off two rounds, hitting him once in the shoulder .He hollered in pain and turned to face her. His face was purple with rage. He shot at her, but his chamber was empty. He swore and threw his gun down.

"Okay. We'll do this the old-fashioned way." He came toward her, and she fired her last round, blasting him in the arm. He yelped and grabbed her around the neck. She bit and kicked him, but he was an iron man, nothing seemed to slow down the steady pummeling from his fists.

She tasted blood, but didn't stop. If she hadn't met Tom, hadn't seen a glimpse of a better life, she might have given up, relieved to have the ordeal of hiding and fear over with. But now, she had something to fight for, to live for, to return home to, and Eden Wyatt wasn't going to let anyone win until she'd breathed her last breath.

At the next blow to her stomach, Eden closed her fingers around Blake's biceps and pulled it to her mouth. She bit down hard, breaking the skin, her teeth sinking into his flesh. He yelled and tried to pull away. Sickened by the taste of his blood, Eden let go. She pushed up and made it through the door. The halls were smoky, and the fire raged on. She ran toward the back door in the kitchen, but Blake lunged, flying through the air and tackling her. She landed with a thud, and her head banged down hard on the tile floor.

Woozy, Eden shut her eyes then opened them to see Blake standing above her. The banging on the wall grew louder.

Marshalling all her strength, she forced her brain to function. "What are you going to do if those guys get out? Do you think they're gonna let you live?'

Blake put his boot on her throat. "I'll be long gone by then, and so will you." He coughed as smoke snaked into the room.

Being on the floor, Eden was beneath the threat of asphyxiation from the smoke, which curled upward, and could still breathe. "Who are you working for?" She raised her gaze to his, barely able to squeak out the words.

"Fuck off." He kicked her then crouched low to avoid the smoke that was growing thicker by the minute.

Another kick to the ribs, and the pain forced Eden into unconsciousness.

* * * *

"Post, Platt, Alexander, Martin, get your shit and get ready, our orders came through. We're rescuing a CIA agent trapped in Beirut. We leave in ten mikes," Colonel Davis barked his commands.

"Aye, sir,"

At 0900, the MV-22B Osprey chopper left the camp. It took an hour and a half to get to Beirut. The plan was to drop the men just outside Beirut, where a Humvee was waiting to get them within two blocks of the target. They would use the cover of the buildings to approach unseen. Fortunately, this was a residential section, and at this time of the day, there weren't many people out and about. After moving in one block, Sergeant Post separated and moved to the third structure's stairwell to his sniper's position.

Davis, Platt, and Alexander kept moving to the house. Each took their respected positions until the set time. At 1030 on the mark, Post and Martin tossed two stun grenades in. Tom and Platt kicked in the front door as planned. A man in dishdasha fired at them as they entered.

Alexander popped out two shots, one in the chest followed by one in the head, dropping the enemy immediately. Two more assassins came out of the room on the left and started shooting. Post and Martin ducked behind a couch and shot back. Both assassins hit the ground, dead.

"Holy shit. Where the hell did they come from?" Post asked.

"Damned if I know. Somebody fucked up."

Alexander and Davis moved to the door on the left while Martin and Platt moved to the one on the right. In the room, Davis saw a man about to shoot someone tied in a chair. Davis raised his pistol and fired, dropping him immediately. Alexander shot at something to Davis' left. He turned to see another man go down. "Clear!" Alexander shouted, and they heard echoes of "Clear!" from the other room.

Moving to the figure in the chair, Davis felt for a pulse. A faint one. He started assessing her injuries. Two black eyes, one almost swollen shut. Her left hand was crumpled, probably a few broken fingers. Mousy brown hair matted over her face with blood drying around the lips and nose. *"Who would do this to a woman?"* ran through his mind before he spoke. He needed to get the code from her to be certain she was the CIA Agent.

"U.S. Marines. You're safe now. What's your grandmother's dog's name?"

"Fluffy."

"What's your name?"

"Eden Wyatt."

"Eden? What the hell—" His blood chilled.

Tom didn't finish, as Eden interrupted him. "Bedroom wall. Hidden room. More people. Blake. Traitor." Her body went limp. She had passed out. Davis cut the rope holding her to the chair, lifted her up, and slung her over his shoulder. He followed his men, his gun in his free hand, ready to provide back-up.

"I'm on it," Alexander said as he and Martin, drawn to the sound of banging, located the hidden room and the entrance. Kicking it open, Martin tossed in a CS Grenade. Immediately, four men came out firing. Two fell over dead from Martin and Alexander's counterattack. The other two were killed by Post's sniper rifle.

"Thank you, Post," Alexander said over the comms.

"I couldn't let you have all the fun," came the reply. "Eight assassins. More than intel told us. Better check for more."

Searching the rest of the house, they found another man hiding in a closet. Alexander raised his weapon to fire.

"Wait! I'm an American."

Keeping his finger on the trigger, Alexander asked, "Who are you?"

"Blake. I work for the CIA. I'm undercover."

Relaxing his trigger finger, Alexander lowered his weapon. "Come on."

Blake grabbed some discs off the desk, shoving them in his pocket.

Then, Tom saw Blake draw his pistol, aiming for Eden. The Lieutenant Colonel shoved Eden out of the way, then he felt a stinging pain in his arm. Suddenly, Blake dropped the gun and fell over, a bullet hole in his right shoulder.

Alexander approached him, grinning, with his weapon drawn. "Didn't know about our sniper, I guess."

"We're taking him back alive. I want to interrogate him. Then, we'll see he spends the rest of his life in prison for treason."

Tom keyed his comm. "Once again, thank you, Post."

"I'll cover you. Meet back at the Hummer in thirty."

"Roger that."

The streets were alive with people moving about trying to find out what was going on. The team moved as quickly as possible, but carrying Eden and pulling Blake slowed them down. Once back at the Hummer, they took off quickly, heading back to the chopper.

Post retrieved a first aid kit from the vehicle and wrapped Tom's arm while the Hummer sped them to safety. Eden was spread across the seat with her head in the lieutenant's lap. Tom's fingers stroked her lifeless cheek.

"Is she gone, sir?" Post asked.

Tom placed two fingers on the base of her neck. "There's a pulse. A weak one, but it's there. Got to get her to the hospital." His eyes watered.

"You know her, sir?"

Tom nodded. "Might say that." Visions of his beautiful lover frolicking on the beach in St. Thomas flashed through his mind. He recalled the feel of her small palm on his bare chest. A shudder flashed through him. He stared at the broken woman lying before him, unrecognizable, her beauty smashed to bits. His heart pounded. *Live, Eden. Live. Come back to me.*

"Like that, is it?"

"Yeah. It is."

Post elbowed Blake hard in the ribs for good measure.

Chapter Twelve

Military hospital in Germany

Colorful visions, like a kaleidoscope, blended and danced through Eden's brain. Dark green, khaki, and the bright orange of flames. She coughed as the image of gray smoke passed through her mind's eye. She tossed in her narrow bed. Discomfort grew as swelling bloated parts of her body. Panic filled her chest as she felt trapped in a bizarre, garish fun house at an amusement park, and there was no way out. She gulped air.

A crash, like the sound of plates smashing on the floor, jolted her awake.

Though she tried to open her eyes, only one cooperated. The other was swollen shut. Her mind was hazy, her vision blurry. *Drugs. I'm on drugs.* Voices came at her as if she were under water. She tried to remember where she had been. Reaching around, she touched her upper arm and was stopped by a bandage there. Bright light stabbed her eye, so she shut it. A cool cloth on her head caused her to open again, but the faces around her were unclear and unfamiliar. She didn't know them. She wasn't even sure she knew herself.

"Eden Marie Wyatt. 031-44-8703," she mumbled through a mouth as dry as sawdust before she fell back to sleep. Darkness washed over her, bringing relief from the stimulation so acute as to be painful. *I'm alive. I'm alive. I'll deal with it all later.* She relaxed and let the medication knock her out. Tension melted out of her body like butter in the sun. She formed a tiny smile with lips split by dryness and puffy from beating.

The murmur of voices nearby woke her again. She had no idea what time it was or what day. She cracked her good eye open and saw the window. Night was creeping in. The sky was lit up with a brilliant sunset. Or was it sunrise? She didn't know. When she moved, pain broke through her meds. She cringed, scrunching up her face, as she rolled onto her back. She bumped a knee into the side railing of the bed and cried out.

The voices stopped. People were at her bedside, asking questions, but she couldn't sort out the words. She waved her arms to make them go away, and it worked. They backed up. Tears slipped out of her eyes as loneliness and fear constricted her chest. A tissue gently wiped away the wetness. She sighed, closed her eye, and tried to get comfortable as the pain subsided. Long, strong fingers closed over hers.

"Eden," a deep, masculine voice whispered.

Tom. The vision of her lover pushed out the evil pictures in her brain. She tried to smile, but it hurt too much, so she stopped. In her mind, she watched him playing on the beach in St. Thomas with her, and her heart filled with warmth.

His hand held hers, but not too tightly. She closed her fingers around his and pressed with the little strength she still possessed. Contentment filled her, and she drifted off again.

The smell of food woke her next time. The swelling of her right eye had receded enough for her to open it. She blinked both eyes and raised her hand to shield them from the sunlight pouring in the window. Her stomach rumbled. For the first time, she noticed how empty it was as hunger gnawed at her innards. She pushed on her hands to sit up, but pain rocketed through her arm.

One glance told her that she had broken fingers. Her splinted and taped left hand made it hard to sit up.

"Do you want to sit up? Are you hungry?" a familiar female voice asked.

Tara. Eden nodded. Suddenly, the head of the bed began to rise, and she was sitting up.

Tara maneuvered a tray over her lap. "Can you feed yourself, or do you need help?"

Despite the swelling, Eden managed a small smile as she stared at her friend. Placing her right hand on the fork, she closed her fingers around it and managed to scoop up some food. But she misjudged the distance to her mouth and spilled the meat on her chest. Tara jumped up and quickly cleaned the mess. Then, she scooped up more and fed it to Eden.

The meat was followed by mashed potatoes. The warm food chased away a chill in her bones. It was like a soothing massage. Still woozy from the potent drugs, Eden was grateful for her friend's care and thankful Tom wasn't there to see her so helpless.

"Tom is coming by again later."

Eden shook her head. "No. I look awful. No. No Tom." She tried to speak clearly through swollen lips, but she was sure that Tara could hardly understand her.

"He's already been here, seen you. He's the one who carried you out of the burning building. He doesn't care what you look like."

Some of the events from her mission came back to her. The feel of his arms around her returned. Tears managed to slip from Eden's eyes. *He saved me.* She reached for the Styrofoam cup next to her bed. Tara grabbed it and steadied it. Eden took a long drink from the straw. The water helped her speak. "I don't want him to see me like this." She wiped her face with the back of her good hand.

"He already has. He loves you, Eden." Tara handed her friend a tissue.

Eden plucked at her short hair. The tears continued.

A nurse came by. "She's pretty upset. Perhaps you'd better go."

"I didn't mean to upset her. I only told her that her boyfriend would be coming by later."

Eden continued to weep.

The nurse shot a sympathetic look at Tara and took Eden's hand. "We'll get you fixed up before he comes. You'll see. You'll look fine," the woman in white told her. She turned to Tara. "Do you know what time he's due?"

Tara checked her watch. "I think about eight."

The nurse smiled. "Good. That gives us plenty of time to get her looking good. Does she have a gown of her own?"

Tara nodded. "Here's her bag."

"Ah. You're a good friend. Why don't you go for coffee, and I'll get her ready for company."

Tara left the room. The nurse pulled the curtain around Eden's bed for privacy. "You'll have to get back into the hospital gown after he leaves, but no harm in you wearing something of your own for an hour tonight." She fished around in the bag and drew out a revealing, pink gown with spaghetti straps.

Eden again attempted a smile.

"Wow. This is pretty hot. Think he can take it?" The nurse grinned.

"He's pretty hot," Eden replied, speaking slowly and carefully. It hurt to talk.

"Let's take our time here," she said, easing the hospital gown down. "Can you lift your arms above your head, so I can slip this on?"

Eden sucked in air and squeezed her eyes shut against the pain. *Broken ribs. That's familiar.*

The nurse slipped the sexy nightie down over Eden and straightened it. "That's one hundred percent better already. What else have you got in this bag of tricks?"

Tara returned with a cup of coffee and helped the nurse gently apply light makeup and lipstick to Eden's bruised face. They brushed her hair and dabbed on a little perfume. The nurse held up a mirror, and Eden's curiosity got the better of her fear. She peeked at herself and let out a gasp when she saw the damage.

Her face was battered and bruised. Her swollen eyelid looked angry. The other was black and blue. Her lower lip was puffy. A few purple splotches mottled her skin. Her hair looked like straw, still the ugly, washed out, light brown color instead of her natural blonde. It was chopped off abruptly a little below her ear.

"I look horrible. Tell him not to come. Please. I'm begging you," Eden said, pulling on Tara's arm.

Tara turned to see Tom standing in the doorway. "Too late."

"Eden?"

She looked at him then fiddled with her nightgown, adjusting the neckline, picking at the trim.

His left arm rested in a sling. "Can I come in?"

She nodded, fighting back tears. "What happened to you?"

"Nicked by a bullet. I'm okay." He took off the sling, folded it up, and stuffed it in his pocket. "I don't really need this, but it relieves some of the pressure."

He walked slowly toward her. She glanced up and made contact with his eyes. She saw them water. He sat in a chair and pulled it close to the bed. Tara got up and left. Eden patted the mattress and inched over slowly to make room. Tom eased himself down next to her. He raised his hand and gently palmed her cheek.

"I almost lost you," he said, his voice cracking.

She touched his face. He leaned down and brushed his lips lightly over hers.

"Thank you for saving me."

He smiled at her. "I didn't recognize you."

Eden winced. "I know I don't look the same." She cast her gaze to her lap.

"I didn't know you'd changed your appearance."

"I'm ugly," she croaked, looking out the window.

"You're *not* ugly. Never. You're beautiful." He stroked her hair.

"And I failed."

"You were sabotaged. You were so brave. I'm proud of you."

"How can you be proud of me? I'm a disaster." Tears spilled down her cheeks.

He pulled out his handkerchief and wiped her face. She cringed.

"I'm sorry. I'm trying to be gentle."

"I didn't do anything."

"You kicked major butt, lady. Your warning was in time for us to take out all the assassins and their reinforcements. If you hadn't done that, they'd have gotten away, and you'd be dead."

She gave a lopsided smile.

"We got that bastard, Blake, too."

"And Sherman?"

"I'm sorry. He was gone when we arrived."

"Thought so. But I don't trust my memory right now."

Tom picked up her left hand. The first two fingers were splinted and taped together. But the third was unharmed. He reached into his pocket and pulled out the diamond ring he had bought her, sliding it on.

"You can wear it now. Besides, I don't want any guys here coming on to you."

She made a face. "The way I look?"

"It won't be long before the swelling is gone and the bruises are healed. I want them to know you're mine." He rubbed the strap of her gown between his fingers.

"Tom," she murmured as she fell into his chest, resting her cheek against his starched uniform. He closed his arms around her. *I could stay like this forever.*

"I don't know what I'd do if you hadn't made it," he whispered, then kissed her hair.

"I love you, too, Davis," she sighed.

"Back to Davis?"

"Oh. Sorry. Tom." She tried to smile.

"That's better."

He stroked her back as he spoke quietly of their future together. "We'll get a house. Just you and me. You can decorate it any way you want. You can work or stay home. Be whatever you want, as long as you're mine, honey."

Eden closed her eyes, soothed by the warmth of his hand, his body against hers, and his soft words of love. The pain dulled as she allowed him to cradle her and turned her thoughts to a happy life with him. *Is it possible? Can I leave this darkness behind?*

The nurse entered. "I'm sorry to break this up, but it's time for her medicine and visiting hours are almost over."

Tom pushed to his feet and stepped back. Eden swallowed the pills before taking his hand with her uninjured one. They laced fingers.

"A few more minutes, colonel. I'm sure you understand."

He nodded and returned to the bed. Eden touched his face, and he lowered his lips to hers. The slight sting from the gentle pressure dissolved into pleasure quickly.

"Get better fast, baby," he muttered into her hair. "Don't think I can take being this close to you and not making love."

She smiled and winced at the same time. "Always horny."

"When you're around." He grinned.

"So, it's my fault?"

"Damn right." Tom glanced at his watch. "It's time, beautiful."

She nodded. One last kiss, and he was gone.

Exhaustion claimed her. Before the nurse could get her changed back to the hospital gown, Eden had fallen into a troubled sleep.

* * * *

Lugging her backpack with a prescription for painkillers tucked into her fist, Eden eased herself into the seat of the Jeep.

Even the slightest bump in the road made her broken ribs sting. She sucked up the pain and smiled at the prospect of the R and R awaiting her.

After only a few days in the hospital, the doctors had judged there to be no serious internal injury, and she had been discharged even though the concussion she had received had short-circuited her memory. Sumner had given her the green light for two weeks to recoup, so Eden was heading back to St. Thomas. Due to his taking a bullet, Lt. Colonel Tom Davis had a week off as well. They would rendezvous at Mick and Tara's place.

She twisted the ring on her finger as her thoughts turned to Tom. *Will this be the beginning of a happy life with him?* Doubt clouded her mind. While her body was recovering nicely and the bruises were beginning to fade, her memory was still cloudy. Something nagged at her, and she couldn't sort it out.

Settled in a window seat on the military transport, Eden was congratulated by others on the part she had played in wiping out the assassins and uncovering terrorists. She blushed at the praise she considered unearned. *I don't deserve credit. I had to call for help and get rescued.* As the plane became airborne, she turned her mind to more pleasant thoughts. She chuckled as she wondered how she and Tom would manage to make love, considering their wounds.

Although desire was beginning to creep back into her body, she didn't care if they didn't make love. All she wanted was to sleep in the same bed with him, bundled into his embrace, safe and warm together. She sat back, relaxed, and closed her eyes, hoping to sleep for much of the long flight to Washington. There, she'd hop a commercial flight, and within three hours, be digging her toes into the whitest sand in the world.

As she slept, fractured pictures of the mission filled her head. Snatches of conversation with Blake and Sherman didn't seem to mean much. Actions in the burning house blended together until they were like a bowl of spaghetti, no image distinguishable from another. She shifted in her seat as the flashing of pictures got scary. A gun blast, the smoke and flames, a foot on her neck. She began to gag in her sleep and awoke with a start.

Sweaty and trembling, she gulped air. She scanned her surroundings. A colonel pushed to his feet and sank down in the empty seat next to her.

"Are you all right?" he asked, his brows knitted.

"I think so. Bad dream. Thank you, sir."

He nodded and returned to his own seat.

Gotta figure out what happened. I can't move on yet. This isn't finished. Someone turned on me. Who and why?

Her mind filled with unanswered questions. She knew her safe future with Tom would have to wait. She had to sort out what had happened and find the mole, or she could never rest, never be safe, and never have a life. Besides, Tom would be threatened, too. That thought made her shiver. Again, she twisted the ring on her hand as she wondered if she should end it with him now before he was dragged into her nightmare.

A layover in Washington gave her time to buy a book. She tried to read as she waited to board the next flight, but her anxiety about safety interrupted her concentration. She still couldn't pinpoint what went amiss, but she sensed she was getting closer. Questions kept circling, but the answers eluded her.

It was dark by the time she landed in Charlotte Amalie. The stewardess woke her, but sleep had not refreshed Eden. Her body ached, and she needed a soft bed like an alcoholic needs a drink. She stumbled down the stairs, gripping her backpack with all her strength.

Mick and Tara were waiting as close to the plane as they could get. Eden pasted a feeble smile on her lips and collapsed into Mick's arms.

Her friends put her to bed. It was dark when she awoke, and she was hungry. She had been asleep for twenty-four hours. Finally, her energy had returned. Feeling better than she had in a long time, Eden got up and slipped on a pair of shorts and a T-shirt. She padded barefoot out to the living room. Tara and Mick were cuddled together on the sofa, watching a movie.

"Eden, you're up." Tara rushed to engulf her in a big hug.

"It's damn rude to die as a guest in someone's home," Eden said.

Mick laughed. "Okay, we admit we checked to see if you were breathing a couple of times."

"How are you?" Tara stepped back, her gaze scrutinizing her friend.

"I've been better, but been worse, too. I'm okay. Finally feeling a bit like me. But I'm starved. I hate to be a pain, but..."

"Come on. We saved you some dinner." Tara took Eden's arm and led her into the kitchen.

* * * *

Early Saturday morning, Tara dyed Eden's hair back to her natural blonde shade. After they ate, Eden finished the breakfast dishes, wiped her hands on the apron she wore, and hung it on a hook by the door. She tucked the newspaper under her arm and went outside. The warm, Caribbean air caressed her face. She sighed. *Tom arrives tomorrow.* She smiled as she eased into a lounge chair.

Mick joined her, occupying the other chaise in the shade.

"This sun is wicked. Be careful," he cautioned.

Eden moved closer to him. "After everything else, I sure as hell don't need a sunburn."

Mick chuckled. "Tom's plane gets in at nine tomorrow morning."

"I can't wait," she said, grinning.

"I'll bet. How long has it been?"

"Too long." She twisted the ring on her finger as her thoughts turned to him. The motion was becoming a habit.

"We're getting a hospital bed for our guest room."

"Seriously?"

"Kidding."

She laughed. *God, it feels good to laugh.* "Where's Tara?"

"Putting her suit on."

Eden's gaze scanned the horizon. She was safe here, at least for the time being. Tom would be there tomorrow morning, early. Her heart rate kicked up at the idea. Closing her eyes, she could almost smell his unique scent and feel his hands on her body. Her fingers itched to touch him, feel the roughness of his uniform then the smoothness of his skin.

"Somebody's off dreaming of something sexy. That look on your face, Miss Eden. Whew. It's heating up the whole deck."

Eden cracked her eyelids to see Tara plop down into a chair on the other side of Mick. He leaned over and kissed her. *I love how they can't keep their hands off each other. I hope Tom and I will be like that.*

"I see something I haven't seen before," Tara sang.

"Huh?"

"Show me your left hand," she ordered.

Eden extended her arm and wiggled her last two fingers, which weren't bandaged.

"Hey, I didn't notice that," Mick said, pulling her hand closer so that he could examine the ring. "That old son-of-a-bitch has better taste than I thought."

"It's beautiful," Tara added. "When's the wedding?"

"Wedding? Damn, we're just trying to stay alive."

"Get married here, on the beach," Tara suggested.

"I have some loose ends to clear up. When my memory comes back all the way, then I'll know what to do."

"That reminds me. I got a fax yesterday. Some intel Tom requested. We should wait to go over it when he's here."

"Good. I'm not sure I'll be much help. I can't seem to remember exactly what happened in Beirut."

"This is all about stuff that happened before."

"I'm pretty clear about the past."

"Good."

Too restless to read for long, Eden relinquished the newspaper to Mick and walked along the beach. She looked for shells and waded in the clear, aqua surf to watch tiny, brilliantly-colored fish dart from place to place, seeking food. She tried to force her brain to bring up what happened in Beirut, but it was useless. *Mind needs a rest.*

She took a deep breath and ran into the ocean. A quick swim and floating near the shore calmed her. She gazed at the palm trees fluttering slightly in the gentle breeze. She spied wind surfers waiting for the wind to pick up and parents with kids, searching for shells on the shore.

Her mind turned to the idea of her wedding. To avoid stress, she focused on the type of dress she should wear. She closed her eyes and saw Tom in full dress uniform, waiting at the altar for her. She envisioned herself in a lacy, strapless dress then a clingy, white, jersey dress with cap sleeves and plunging neckline.

She wondered what sage advice her Gram would give her. She knew the older woman would approve of a Marine Lieutenant Colonel...as long as he was good to Eden. Colonel Davis was the gold standard for men. He treated her like a queen, but never stopped being a man.

She stretched her lips into a smile as she let her mind roam with happy thoughts. Her swellings had receded, and her face was almost back to normal color. The bruises on her body were still prominent, but she hoped that wouldn't matter too much to Tom. *If he's horny enough, he won't care if my skin is green.* She chuckled.

Eden returned in time to help Tara with lunch. She set the table on the deck, sneaking peeks at the loving couple. Mick was standing behind Tara, his arms around her. His head was bent. Tara stopped fussing at the cutting board and eased her neck back. Mick took the hint and kissed down the slim column. One glance at the muscles working in his arms gave Eden an idea of what his hands were doing.

She blushed and turned away, wishing to give them some privacy. She chuckled to herself that, after lunch, they'd find some excuse to steal away and be alone. Sure enough, after the sandwiches and iced tea were consumed, Tara stretched her arms and announced that she planned to take a nap. Mick disappeared shortly after.

Eden sat under the shade of a coconut tree and read a romance novel. Right now, she needed all the happy endings she could get.

* * * *

Feeling like a teenager awaiting her first date, Eden couldn't stop her pulse from leaping. She sat in the back as Mick drove them to the airport. Tom's plane was due to land in five minutes. Eden replenished her lipstick for the third time since she had gotten in the car. She fluffed her hair for the second time. Then, she shifted from left to right in the back seat.

"He's coming. Take it easy," Mick said, looking at her in the rear view mirror.

"I know how she feels," Tara put in.

"Sorry. I don't mean to be a pain."

Mick pulled up to the curb. The women got out, and Eden rushed inside. She was restrained by security. As she watched the aircraft taxi down the runway toward the building, her heart pounded. *He'll be here in less than five minutes.*

Before she could take another breath, she spied him at the top of the stairs. With one arm in a sling, he balanced his duffel on his opposite shoulder and took his time on the steep steps.

Her eyes stared, focused on his every movement. He looked so incredibly handsome in his uniform, simply looking at him made her tingle all over. Soon, she'd be in his arms and life would be good.

When his gaze connected with hers, he grinned and picked up the pace, almost running to get to her. He scooped her up in the air with one arm and squeezed her too tight. She yelped, and he loosened his grip.

"Sorry. I forgot. Ribs. You look amazing. Back to your old self."

"Almost."

She looked up into his eyes, and his lips came down on hers for a hungry kiss. Everything inside Eden fluttered as he took her mouth, holding her against him. She melted into his embrace, wanting more, but holding back, as they were in a public place. They broke long enough for Tom to shake Mick's hand and give Tara a hug. Mick grabbed the duffel, and they piled into the car and headed for home.

When they arrived, there were several faxes waiting for Mick.

"I've got some interesting intel, Tom. We need to talk."

"Can't we give them some time alone, Mick?" Tara fluttered her big eyes at her husband.

"They'll have all night, Tara."

"Let me unpack then we can sit down." Tom picked up his valise.

Mick agreed and the colonel went to his room. Eden followed.

"She's going in there while he unpacks? We won't see them for hours," Mick said.

"I heard that," Eden called after him then broke into a throaty laugh.

"They know us too well," Tom turned to her after placing his bag on the chair. He removed the sling.

"Do you still need that?" she asked.

"Not all the time. But it helps when I'm traveling. Keeps people from bumping into me. I'll be okay in another few days."

"Can you bend it?"

"You mean, can I bend it around you? Let's find out." He pulled her into his chest and folded his arms around her. "Seems to work just fine."

She tipped her chin up to receive his kiss. He slid his hands down to her rear end and squeezed.

"Feels damn good," he muttered into her mouth.

"Umm hmm," she replied.

He glided his hands around her sides and up to rest on her breasts. "Are they sore? Do I have to be careful?"

She wiggled out of her tank top and stood half naked in front of him. "You judge." Her heart rate doubled. *Will he find me ugly?*

He winced as his gaze settled on her bruised flesh. "Ouch. That must have hurt."

"It did. Not so much now." She shrugged.

"How'd it happen?"

"Got kicked." Her facial expression didn't change.

"Damn bastard. I'd like to kill him. Can I touch you at all?"

"Damn well better, or I'll have to shoot you."

He laughed. "I'll be gentle." He placed his palms on her, skimming his fingertips across her smooth skin. "They're beautiful, even with the bruises."

"I think you have a healing touch."

"Why?"

"You're making them tingle."

Tom cracked up. Wrapping his hands around her sides, he eased her into him and held her close, but not too tight.

Eden closed her eyes. "Can I stay like this for maybe…umm…a century?"

"You can stay like this as long as you like, beautiful," he whispered into her hair.

She looked into his eyes and saw the love behind them. She believed that he would spend the rest of his life with her, if she let him.

Chapter Thirteen

"I don't think they're coming out for a while." Mick glanced at the closed door as he gathered up the faxes and put them in the order in which they had arrived.

"You think they're fooling around?" Tara stopped taking meat out of the freezer.

Mick cocked an eyebrow at Tara. "If that was us, what would we be doing?"

"Oh. Guess you're right." She laughed and continued to gather food to defrost for dinner.

Mick put the papers down and approached his wife. He put his hands on her waist.

She slid her hands up his hard chest. "They're giving me ideas."

He drew her closer.

She raised her chin and nuzzled his neck.

"Whoo hoo. Angel, when you do that..." His arms tightened around her.

"When I do what?" She planted tiny kisses on him.

"What you're doin'. Wow, gets me going."

She sighed and slipped her fingers under his T-shirt. "What were we talking about?"

"I have no idea." Mick scrunched up his face as her fingers combed through his chest hair. "Damn, honey." He closed his eyes for a moment, but she didn't stop. "I'm trying to remember. Oh, yeah. I was gonna ask you...about when you're well again."

"Yeah."

"Are you?"

"I think so. The PTSD seems to be going away. I only have a few bad dreams. Probably don't have more because I'm sleeping next to you." She pushed his shirt up, and he ripped it over his head and tossed it on a chair.

"If we have to save Eden, do you want to help?" He combed his fingers through her long, auburn locks.

"I do." She slurped a lick along his pecs.

He shivered. "And you're okay? I don't want you to freak out or get hurt." He bent to kiss her neck.

"As long as you're there. Yeah." She leaned back and closed her eyes.

He kissed down the vee of her shirt. "I think Tom and Eden need us."

"Do you?" Her breath came faster, and she opened her eyes.

"I do." He cupped her breast, revealed by the deep neckline, and kissed the top.

She ground her hips into his. "They've got to get this settled, or they'll never have a life."

"So, it's okay? You're in? I don't want to push you." He flicked her peak with his thumb.

She gasped then took a breath. "I love you, Mick. I want to be part of the team. I'm in."

"You're amazing. I love you, too, angel."

Tara looked up at him, and he lowered his mouth to hers for a kiss. A tiny moan escaped her, and Mick deepened it. Tara pushed against him, her breasts crushed into his chest. He slid one hand down to cup her bottom then moved his fingers to her inner thigh.

"Angel, I could take you right here," he muttered, stroking her through her shorts.

"They could reappear any time." Her breathing was ragged, and she leaned against him.

Mick stepped back, rubbing his hands on his wife's sides. "You're the sexiest thing. You know that?"

"Glad you think so." She took a deep breath and slowly backed away, putting a little distance between them. "Let's talk first." Tara sat down at the table.

"Is it hot in here?"

"That's just you. You're naturally hot."

"There you go again. Better stop or I won't be able to concentrate." He joined her.

She grinned at him. "Tell me what you want to do."

"I've looked over these faxes and there seem to be two possible moles."

"Two?"

"Yep. Two. We need to smoke out the right one."

"Do you have a plan?"

"We need some information from Eden and Tom, too. Once we have that, I'm sure we can develop one that'll work."

"We're going to be together forever." She drew his hand to her mouth.

"I couldn't live without you." He cupped her cheek.

She turned to kiss his palm. "Me, neither."

"They deserve the same chance we've had."

"They do." She stood up and settled in his lap.

"And we're going to help them get it. Right?" He slipped his fingers under her shirt and closed them around her breast.

"Right." She sighed.

"Those bad guys need to be eliminated." He circled her nipple.

"They do. True love'll win," she said, her voice coming in small pants.

Mick moved his hand down to rest on her thigh. Tara looked in his eyes and kissed him. He dipped his fingers under the fabric of her shorts and moved them up slowly. She drew in a breath as they hit home. She parted her legs. He stroked her as he nibbled on her collarbone.

"Damn, Mick," Tara breathed, her eyes closed, her fingers curled around his erection.

Mick withdrew, eased her off his lap, and stepped back. Tara reached for his hand.

"Come on, angel." He led her into the bedroom and shut the door.

* * * *

Eden and Tom opened their door first. She padded into the kitchen, turned to Tom, and raised her eyebrows. He glanced toward the other bedroom.

"Their door is closed," he said.

Eden chuckled. "Guess love is in the air."

Tom opened the fridge and grabbed two beers. He twisted the tops off and handed one to Eden.

"Might as well get lunch started while they're…uh…busy." Eden opened a loaf of bread.

"I'll set the table."

Twenty minutes later, the door to Mick and Tara's bedroom opened. The husband and wife trotted out, holding hands. When they entered the kitchen, they stopped short. The two couples stood face to face. Eden's hand was poised with a knife full of mayonnaise. Tom was putting a plate on the table.

"Bet you're hungry. How about lunch?" Eden asked to break the tension. After a second, the kitchen was filled with laughter. Tara made a pitcher of iced tea, and Mick grabbed two more beers.

When they were finished, Tom brought up the subject first. "Any interesting intel, Mick?"

Tara left the room. She returned with a handful of papers. "Here's the stuff from the fax."

Tom and Mick read the documents quietly while Tara and Eden cleared the table.

"Interesting," Tom said. "Eden, you slept with Sumner? You never mentioned that."

"I didn't think it mattered. It was ages ago."

"He might be jealous, or pissed off and want to retaliate."

"Guys get jealous all the time. They don't try to kill you. Besides, he didn't seem upset at the time. We didn't really have that much going on. No chemistry."

"For you or him? *He* may have thought you had chemistry."

"True. I thought he was actually relieved. Sumner's always been kind of a loner. He knew I was seeing Jerry. You think he's the one?"

"Might have wanted to kill Jerry."

"Jerry? Yeah. Could be. But why me?"

"If he suspected you'd figured it out…then, yeah, you."

"You really think Sumner is a possibility?"

"Maybe. Let's look at Lynn."

Eden blew out a breath. "Wow. I had no idea her daughter, Rosemary, was dating Jerry. I knew he'd just broken up with someone before we started going out, but I didn't know who."

"Let's look at a different scenario. Lynn blames Rosemary's suicide on Jerry. So, she leaks his whereabouts to the family of the guy he got killed." Tom sipped his beer.

"That would work," Mick said.

"But what about Eden? Why kill her?" Tara asked.

"Maybe she sees me as the reason Jerry left Rosemary," Eden piped up.

"Were you?" Tom asked, his gaze resting on her face.

"Jerry said his previous girlfriend was too clingy. I thought he'd dumped her before we went out."

"I bet Lynn didn't know that." Tara opened a box of cookies.

"Probably not," Mick said.

"Jerry and I were friends for about six months before we started dating. He'd complain about his girlfriend, but never mentioned her name."

"Did Lynn know you were dating Jerry?" Tom asked.

"I don't think so. But she found out when Jerry got killed and I got snatched. After Sumner had me rescued, the truth came out about how I was kidnapped."

"So, Lynn found out you were with Jerry…his girlfriend," Tom said.

Eden nodded.

"That might have given her motive to take you out," Mick took two chocolate chip cookies.

"Sick mind." Tara shook her head.

"Maybe after she found out about you, she figured she'd killed the wrong person," Tom said.

"That is definitely a possibility. Blaming you for her daughter's suicide, she wants you dead." Mick passed the plate to Tom.

"Or it could be Sumner," Tara reminded the group.

"We still haven't narrowed it down." Eden grabbed a chocolate chip.

"It's gotta be one of them. Let's set a trap." Tom put the plate down in front of Tara.

"Ideas, Mick?" Tara took the last one.

"We nabbed Blake's phone. I think I've still got it," Tom said, rising from the table.

"I thought I had it?" Eden looked at him with a question in her eyes.

Tom returned with the mangled cell in his hand. "I found it rummaging through your stuff at the hospital, looking for a brush. It looked totaled, but I threw it in my bag anyway."

"It won't be any good." Tara turned the phone over and over in her hand.

"But they don't know that," Eden said.

Tom rose from the table and began to pace. "How do we set this up? And where?"

"We need to keep you safe." Tara patted her friend's shoulder.

"Damn right. Eden has risked enough. Lucky she's still alive," Tom agreed, running his fingers through his hair.

"Eden, are you sure you want to do this? Wouldn't it be safer to let the guys handle it?" Tara pressed.

Tom straddled his chair and folded his fingers around hers. "Baby, you should stay out of this and get better."

"I have to do it…have to know…for Jerry as well as myself. Gotta confront whoever did this."

"As long as you're sure," Mick said.

"I need to be face to face."

"I understand. Bet Tom does, too." Mick leaned back.

Tom nodded. "I do. I don't like it much, but I understand."

Eden touched his shoulder. "I'll be the bait."

"That's what I don't like. You in danger." Tom cupped her face. "I want you safe."

"Love you for that, Davis. This is the best way to flush them out—offering the phone."

"She's right, Tom. They'll think it'll show their calls to Blake. It's perfect," Mick agreed.

"As long as nothing goes wrong. Still—"

Eden placed her finger on Tom's lips. "I get it. Love you for it. But we've gotta do this. If you're there, I know I'll be okay."

"Damn right, I'll be there." Tom pushed up and resumed pacing.

"We have to do it. Then you two can get on with your lives. Let's get down to the details," Mick said.

Tara added more cookies to the plate on the table and refreshed their drinks.

"They're in D.C. So, we take the operation back to the States." Mick picked up his glass.

"Lure them to one of the abandoned warehouses on Jenkin's Pier. Used to be a temporary safe house," Eden suggested.

"In Grandville, Virginia?" Tom asked.

"Right."

"Fine." Mick sketched the warehouse on the back of the fax. "It all starts with a phone call," Tom said.

The two men looked up. Their eyes met then they turned to glance at Eden.

* * * *

The night before they were to head stateside, the foursome sat outside on the deck, drinking piña coladas. Streaks of orange and pink tinted the sky as day faded into night. They had gone out to dinner as a diversion. Two more days, and they were set to spring their trap and catch a cold-blooded killer.

But tonight was about banter, jokes, and relaxing. Mick and Tom told funny stories about growing up together.

"Then, there was Mary Lou Kallon," Mick said.

"Shut up, Mick."

"Go on," Eden said.

"If you do…" Tom threatened.

"Tom had a crush on her when she was nine. She was pretty cute then."

"Oh?" Eden cocked an eyebrow at the lieutenant colonel.

"Mick, shut the hell—"

"But she paid no attention to him. He even picked wild flowers for her. Of course, he was a year younger."

"Mick, I'm warning you."

"Go on," Eden urged.

"Then, when they were in high school, she became interested in him."

"Mick!"

"But by then, she wasn't cute anymore, and he didn't like her. She asked him to a Sadie Hawkins dance. He couldn't think of an excuse."

"Mick!" Tom rose out of his chair.

"He had to take her. But he bitched about it constantly. Then, she wanted to make out. She was sixteen and had her license. So, she drove them to Chestnut Lane."

"Mick, Goddamn it! Shut up!"

Eden put her hand on his arm, and interrupted, "Then what happened?"

"Tom wouldn't make out with her. She started yelling. Cops came. They got hauled down to the police station. I thought Tom's dad was gonna have a heart attack."

"I told you."

"Too late," Eden said.

"Yeah. People were talking about it for years. Everyone thought Tom had attacked that girl. He didn't go near her again. We celebrated when she graduated and left town."

Tom punched Mick in the arm. "Had to tell that one, didn't you?"

"It's your best story."

"Not the one where I threw the winning pass as quarterback on our final football game?"

"Hell no. That's boring," Mick snickered. "Parking with Mary Lou is much better."

Eden turned to face him. "So, you were a make-out artist in high school?"

"Damn right. Not with Mary Lou, but I did okay. How about you?"

"I never kiss and tell, Davis." Eden patted his cheek.

Learning more about Tom, the man she planned to marry, amused her. She gazed at her engagement ring from time to time to remind herself it was real.

As the pink sunset disappeared into the turquoise of night and the sky darkened, the two couples yawned and stretched, heading for the privacy of their bedrooms. This was Eden's last chance to be alone with Tom before she put herself squarely in the middle of the scheme to lure the bloodthirsty spider. As Tom closed the door, she slipped the band off her finger.

"Please, keep it safe for me."

He nodded and returned it to the tiny, velvet box on the nightstand. They washed up, undressed in silence, and slipped under the covers. Eden plumped up the pillows and added one from the chair at the vanity. She arranged them so she could sleep propped up. She found it painful to rise up from lying flat, so she slept partially sitting. It still hurt to push forward and get out of bed, but this way, it hurt less.

Tom watched her. "Can I help you?"

She shook her head. "I'll get it."

"Do you want to go right to sleep?"

"Oh?" She arched an eyebrow and turned slowly to face him. "Afternoon delight not enough, Davis?"

"It's never enough with you. Just whets my appetite." He chuckled. "It won't be long before you'll have to be calling yourself that, too."

She smiled at him. "I'm sorry. I know you hate it."

"Because I actually like my first name."

"So do I." She inched nearer to him, staring up into his eyes. "Tom."

He combed his fingers through her cropped locks. "Your hair is kinda cute short like this."

"I think you're kinda cute," she countered.

"Cute?" He made a face.

"That's an insult? Women think men are cute all the time."

"No man wants to be called cute. I can think of a dozen other things a man wants to be called."

"How about being called to get his butt over to my side of the bed?"

"Yes, ma'am." Tom skittered closer to her. He snaked one arm around her waist, pulling her up against him. "Does that hurt?"

"Feels good." His warm, firm chest pushed against her breasts. His soft hair there tickled her nipples. Tom splayed his fingers over her back and bent to kiss her. Eden raised a leg and hooked it over his middle.

"Holy hell, if you're gonna do that…" But he lost his words when he lowered his lips to hers again.

Eden's pulse jumped. Surrendering her mouth to his turned her on. He had a way of being commanding without being scary. He wanted her and showed it. She loved that about him. But he never forced her or ignored her if she said something didn't feel good. She wound her arms around his neck and softened against him.

A smile stretched her lips when she realized she trusted him. She hadn't trusted anyone since Jerry, and it felt good. *Damn good.* Her heart opened to him.

His torso heated against hers. A fine layer of sweat formed between them. Their bodies slid apart and together easily. Tom lowered his hand slowly down her leg until he turned it to the vee between her legs.

"Wow," he muttered.

"You take me from zero to a hundred in about thirty seconds," she replied.

His experienced fingers stroked her, hitting the high spots and finding the perfect rhythm. She moved her hips with his movements as the ache to have him inside her became unbearable.

"Damn, Tom. Do it. Take me. God, I'm dying here," she moaned, closing her lips on his shoulder.

He reached a long arm to the nightstand and plucked a condom from the drawer then covered himself quickly. Eden closed her fingers around him and glided him up and down her slippery flesh.

"Oh, God. Don't tease me, baby," he groaned.

She chuckled as she positioned him perfectly. One thrust and he was inside. Eden moaned as her body temperature soared. Nothing made her happier than making love with Tom. He began to move.

"Tell me if I hurt you, babe. I don't know what's sore."

"Where you are right now isn't sore at all."

He laughed and thrust harder.

"Oh, God, do that again," she whispered.

So he did. Soon, he had a rhythm going, and Eden fell right in. She tried to move only her hips, but when her torso got jostled, she gasped in pain.

"You okay?" Tom's brows knit as he looked down on her.

Sweat beaded on her forehead. "Goddam, effing ribs," she muttered.

Tom pushed up on his arms to lessen the weight on her chest. "Better?" He grimaced for a second as a small stab of pain shot up the arm that was grazed by a bullet.

She nodded. *He's the best. I love him so much.*

His hips kept up the pace, and she soon found the heat he was creating in her rising and intensifying to an almost unbearable level. Before she realized it, a huge orgasm washed over her like a tidal wave. She groaned his name and shut her eyes as her muscles tightened. All she could do was feel. His chuckle made her grin.

"Think that's funny?"

"I love it when you come."

"Do you?" Her gaze connected with his.

"Yeah."

"Job well done, eh?" She cocked an eyebrow at him.

"Might say that." He blushed.

"Your turn." She increased the pace, undulating her hips faster and trying to raise her legs. Although the pain in her chest was intense when she shifted to rest her ankles on his shoulders, it wasn't so bad when she pulled her knees to her chest. Tom pounded all the way in, groaning with each push. *He's close.*

Before she could change position, he thrust hard and stopped, muttering her name and closing his eyes. She held him as tight as she could without too much discomfort and planted a kiss on his shoulder.

"I love you, Tom," she whispered.

He raised his head. His eyes connected with hers. She loved the color, like the sky on a cloudless day. "I love you, too, beautiful." He brushed his lips against hers.

"Someday, we'll be together forever."

Tom crouched on his heels and headed for the bathroom. When he returned, he sat back against the four pillows and drew Eden into his embrace. "We need to talk."

"Shoot," she said, turning her gaze to him.

"When this is over and you can have a life again, where do you want to live? Will you stay with the Agency?"

"I've had enough. Where will you be stationed?"

"I don't know yet."

"Can't I live with you?"

"Not if I'm in Afghanistan. But we can apply for a place near Mick and Tara in North Carolina after I do my year in Kings Bay. Would that work for you?"

"As long as I can be with you, I'll be happy."

"What about work?"

"Maybe some private investigation stuff. Or maybe I'll keep house for you, have a kid or two."

His face lit up. "Kids? Really?"

"Yeah. Little Tommy's running around."

"Awesome."

"You want kids?"

"Yeah. I do. Especially a little girl, just like her mom." He stroked her hair.

Eden sensed heat rising to her cheeks as tears watered her eyes. "It's been such a long time since I've had dreams like this. It's wonderful," she whispered.

She cupped his face then snuggled down into his shoulder. He draped his arm around her and closed his eyes.

"Can you sleep like this?"

He cracked an eye to gaze at her. "Hell yeah. You?"

"As long as you're wrapped around me, I can sleep anywhere." She yawned.

"'Night, beautiful."

"'Night, Davis…uh, Tom." But her chuckle gave her away. He swatted her bare behind gently and laughed.

She ran her fingers up his chest, letting her palm rest on his pecs. "Umm, nice."

His hand lay on her rump. "Yeah."

Then, there were no more sounds until morning crept through the curtains.

Chapter Fourteen

Breakfast was a quiet affair. Eden was sad to leave the peace, safety, and beauty of the island, but she knew the necessity of flushing out the mole and getting her life back. Tension over the mission they were about to undertake grew as they prepared to return to the States.

They boarded an early morning flight and arrived in Washington by noon. They rented two cars at the airport and drove to a motel Mick had found within ten miles of the warehouse. The two couples gathered in one of the bedrooms to finalize their mission.

Mick pulled out the drawing of the warehouse, and they went over the plans two more times before they got up to leave. At the door, Eden stopped to check the messages from her cell. She shook her head.

"I thought for sure one of them would ask the condition of the phone or say throw it away. But no. They both want to come and pick it up. So, we still don't know who it is."

"Could it be both of them?" Mick asked.

"I suppose," Eden replied. "But it seems unlikely."

"I guess we'll find out, won't we?" Tom closed the door behind him.

They each took their own car. Tara rode with Mick, who left first. The meeting wasn't scheduled for three hours, but they needed time to set up before they could spring their trap. The plan was for Eden to drive to Grandeville and stop at a diner. She would have a piece of apple pie and coffee. Chatting with the waitress would make her conspicuous, which they wanted.

Mick and Tara arrived at the warehouse first. He unloaded the surveillance equipment from the trunk and pulled out his drawing.

They entered the building and were greeted by the dank smell of age blended with dirt. Tara sneezed. Mick saw the dust in the light filtering through the grungy windows. He looked around, taking in all the features so he could perfect the plan. *No room for mistakes.*

The windows were plentiful, but they were small and high up. There was no way to see inside. Mick frowned. *Not good. Can't have Tara outside with binoculars to call police in case of emergency.*

The floor was cement, stained in some places with paint and others with grease, making it slippery. *Gotta warn Eden to be careful where she steps. If she falls, the plan could fail.* Old wood pallets were stacked on one side. Some were broken, others intact. *Can those pieces of wood be used as weapons? Maybe.* He made a mental note to steer Eden away from there.

In the back, right-hand corner was a flimsy cot covered with a dirty sheet. *Eden's old safe house, eh? Looks pretty disgusting. Maybe it was better back then.* Next to the cot were a half-size refrigerator and a table with a hot plate on it. The hot plate was unplugged, as was the fridge. *Bet the damn thing is full of mold.* His stomach turned for a moment at the thought.

In the left corner was a pile of debris. Crates, boxes, some full, some empty, were rotting in the damp air. Glancing up, he noticed a small loft area. But it was more like a second-story crawl space, as there wasn't enough room for a man his height to stand up. His gaze scanned the room, searching for the locations they'd chosen on his drawing. He spotted the places and nodded to himself. *Yep. Best for the surveillance stuff.*

"You remember the plan?" he asked, as he handed Tara one of the tiny video cameras. She nodded and headed toward the stairs. Mick grabbed another and turned in the opposite direction. About twenty minutes later, they returned to the car. Tom pulled up.

"Both cameras are set up. Let's case the establishment and look for any discrepancies between the blueprints and the actual building."

Tom nodded in agreement, and the three started the inspection. Covering every corner in every room, they familiarized themselves with the warehouse.

"Let's test the cameras. I don't want anything to go wrong," Tom said, pacing.

Mick sent Tara to speak in front of the equipment then he played it back. He placed the earphones on and listened. "She's coming through loud and clear," he reported.

Tom watched the screen. "I can see her okay."

After a hand signal from Mick, Tara moved to the other device and repeated her actions. Mick gave Tom a thumb's up and the lieutenant colonel heaved a sigh.

"Everything's working. Good. Who's taking which position?" Tom asked.

"I know you want to be as close to Eden as possible, Tom. I want you on the main level behind that pile of crates. If the shit hits the fan, you'll be seconds from her. I'll be in the loft with my sniper rifle, covering both of you. And Tara'll be as far away as possible."

Tom nodded in agreement. "We need to keep Tara safe, too."

"I'm putting Tara in our car, parked two warehouses down in the back. We'll be connected by audio. So, if anything goes wrong, she can call the police."

"Perfect. I doubt the mole'll search down there."

"We'll leave your car there, too. Two cars are less suspicious than one."

"I agree," Tom said.

Mick's stomach rumbled. He wasn't sure if he was simply hungry or nervous. Maybe a bit of both. "Let's eat while we have time."

Tom nodded and followed them in his vehicle. They parked at the warehouse where Tara would be stationed then he stuffed himself in the backseat of Mick's car. There was silence in the vehicle as they drove to the diner where Eden was still eating and reading the newspaper.

The threesome sat on the opposite side from her. After a quick glance, she returned to her reading and requested more coffee. Mick sat Tom at a table with his back to Eden, assuming his friend would have a hard time keeping his eyes to himself.

While eating, the conversation revolved around the plan. The cameras would record everything for evidence so that Eden could get her life back, one she planned to spend with Tom. They kept their voices low as they went over every detail.

"You're assuming they'll cop to everything, and we'll have it on tape," Tom said.

"Right," Mick replied.

"But then, they'll try to take out Eden. She's a witness."

"And we step in." Mick took a bite out of his burger.

"Will you have to kill them?" Tara asked.

"I hope not. But we will if we have to," Mick answered, closing his fingers around his wife's hand.

"So, this is dangerous for all of you." Tara pushed her plate away, her omelet barely touched.

"You gotta eat, Tara. I need you fueled up and strong." Mick slipped his arm around her shoulders. "Come on, angel." He pulled the dish back in front of her. She smiled at him and picked up her fork.

Tom lowered his gaze to his plate. "Someone's gotta stop this."

"Might as well be us," Mick said, finishing the thought and his coffee as well.

* * * *

In a comfortable, three bedroom apartment on L Street, Sumner Smith got out of the shower and wound a towel around his hips. He scratched his chest, smiling at the fact that at forty-eight, it was still firm. *The gym has paid off.*

"Coffee's ready," came the call from a female voice.

"Coming, babe," he said. He stroked his cheek and decided he could wait one more day to shave. His girl liked him this way. After a night of heart-stompin' sex, Sumner was relaxed and ready to tackle the most unpleasant task of his career. *She brought it on herself.*

His thoughts turned to the few wild nights he had spent with Eden Wyatt so long ago. He shook his head. *What was I thinking? Now I could be going down with her. And she* will *go down. She killed Jerry, faked her capture, and then tried to kill Blake. I loved you once, Eden, but you're going down, honey.*

He dried himself, thinking back on how many times he had satisfied his girl. *I'm not getting older. I'm getting better.* He chuckled to himself. Being head of his division in the CIA didn't make for many laughs. His job was serious. Many lives depended on his judgment and acumen.

He shook his head, surprised he'd misjudged Eden so badly. *It's not like me to be fooled by a pretty face.* He was a bit ashamed to have committed such a huge error in front of his girlfriend.

Thoughts of Eden left his mind as he smelled two of his favorite aromas, fresh brewed coffee and bacon sizzling in the pan. *Filled one appetite, now on to the next.* She made a wicked goat cheese omelet with a side of bacon, and his mouth watered as he slipped on his boxers and pants. *I'll go bare-chested to the table. Give her a thrill.*

Before he sat down, he stopped to kiss Lynn as she stood by the stove. She turned and was in his arms before he could blink. Her short, blonde hair framed her face perfectly. At forty-seven, she was still pretty and slim. *She gives a great blowjob, too.* He patted her rear end. "I'm starved."

"Your favorite. Coming up." She smiled as she put the plate down in front of him. The food was artfully arranged, with small slices of orange and apple used as decoration. Her attention to detail over breakfast, in the office, and in bed was something he greatly admired.

She returned to the table with her own plate and sat across from him. As they ate, he recalled how they had gotten started. It was after her husband, Hal, had died—about a year after Rosemary had committed suicide. Lynn had come to Sumner in tears. He had wanted to be there for her in her grief because she was his secretary and she was alone.

At first, she had wanted to give him sex as a thank-you for all he'd done—helping her find a smaller, more affordable apartment, giving her more bereavement time off, and keeping her workload light. But Sumner had refused. *That would've been grubby.*

It wasn't long before she had begun to dress differently. It had taken him a couple of weeks to notice her wearing her blouse open at the neck, revealing a little cleavage. She wore tighter skirts, lively print dresses, and she seemed to be bending over more. Was she prettier or was that only him, more aware of her now that she was a widow? It wasn't very long after Hal's death that he had found himself wanting to touch her in lots of inappropriate ways.

While he hadn't acted on those urges, being appalled he even had them, Lynn had picked up on it. She appeared to have a sixth sense about him and made the first move. Sumner had restrained himself and put her off, but she hadn't given up. After a month, however, he had given in. She gave him a blowjob in the office, something he'd vowed would never happen. After that, she had been at his place three nights a week.

Sumner had joined a gym and worked out regularly. He had watched his diet, trimmed down, and bought some more current suits. When his colleagues commented on the change in his appearance, he had simply chuckled, but kept the truth to himself.

Life in the office had improved a hundred fold. Working with his lover brightened his days. Stolen kisses, touches, and squeezes added an air of the forbidden to an otherwise serious occupation. Sumner was charmed by Lynn's sweet thoughtfulness. She had his favorite coffee blend, Kona, on hand and ordered chicken Caesar wrap sandwiches for his lunch. For Valentine's Day, she'd had the drab picture of his parents reframed.

So, when she had come to him with her theory about Eden, he listened. Never a foolish or impulsive man, Sumner took in the facts Lynn laid out. He pondered it long and hard before deciding she had a point. While he couldn't act without hard evidence, his suspicions of Eden grew. Still, when Lynn begged him not to call in the Marines in Beirut, he did anyway. He wasn't about to let lovely, hard-working, traitorous Eden die without a trial.

When Eden'd offered him Blake's cell phone, he jumped at the chance to trap her into admitting who and what she was. A counterspy, a dealer in espionage for the other side…any term he thought of disgusted him equally. He'd trusted Eden with secrets of the United States, and she'd betrayed him and her country. She had to be taken down. The only way was for him to do it. That would exonerate him from his role as a foolish dupe.

Yet, there was a nagging doubt lingering in his gut. This exchange was the perfect place to get at the truth. Sumner planned to wear a wire and trap her into an admission. Then let the Justice Department deal with her. He'd wash his hands of it and put this nasty business behind him. A touch of regret tugged at his heart, but he'd made up his mind.

"I'm stopping at the office before we rendezvous at the warehouse." He snapped his holster on and put his gun in the pouch.

"I'll meet you there then." She cleared the table.

"Right. Love you," he said, kissing her.

"Love you, too," Lynn replied.

Sumner Smith shrugged his suit jacket over his shoulders and flipped his car keys out of his pants pocket. He took the stairs, whistling a march by John Philip Souza.

* * * *

Lynn Wesmore washed the dishes and put them in the drainer to dry. Then, she sat back in a comfortable living room chair in Sumner's place and finished her coffee. Soon her plan would be in motion and all the aggravation of the past two years would be over. She took a deep breath and released it slowly.

She'd waited a long time for this. *Finally, revenge on Eden Wyatt. It's about fucking time.*

She smiled, but didn't feel happy inside. *What the hell am I going to do with Sumner?* She lifted her legs to rest on the coffee table and closed her eyes. *Bet I could get him to marry me. Do I want that? It was bad enough being married to Hal.*

Bitterness welled up inside Lynn when she thought about Rosemary. *Shit, I still miss you, kid.* She remembered her own teenage dreams. Lynn hadn't wanted to get married, ever. She was going to have a career, be a spy, then write a book, make it into a movie, and play the starring role. She'd had plans, big ones, and they hadn't included marriage or motherhood.

Lynn came from a small town. She had lived in a trailer with her mother. She had watched her mother's dreams evaporate under the stress of supporting and raising a family by herself. Her dear mother had worked night and day, but it had never seemed to be quite enough. They had always been scratching to make ends meet.

Lynn had hated her life. She had found escape in sex. Boys made her feel like a goddess, beautiful, important. So, she'd put out and they'd come running. Then, she had one passionate night unprotected and got pregnant. Hal had offered to marry her. Lynn couldn't bring disgrace down on her overburdened mother, so she'd accepted.

Never a love match, Lynn and Hal had found something in common with the birth of their daughter. Rosemary was a beautiful, obedient child. As motherhood took over and Lynn watched her dreams die, they became reborn in her daughter. She began grooming the girl to win beauty contests, spelling bees...anything that would get attention.

Rosemary had been on her way to a modeling career. Or so Lynn had thought. Until the young woman met Jerry. It had been love at first sight for Rosemary—she couldn't talk about anything else. Hal took it well, but not Lynn. *Another man interfering with my dream.* Hal encouraged his daughter to date Jerry, who appeared to be a fine man with a good career. Lynn wanted more for her girl. They argued constantly. Rosie threatened to move in with Jerry.

Lynn had been heartsick. But when Rosemary came home heart-broken and told her mother that Jerry didn't want to live with her and, in fact, had broken up with her, Lynn's dreams rose again. She didn't know how much in love Rosemary was with the handsome agent. Until Rosemary jumped off the bridge.

Hal had been beside himself. So, Lynn had done him a favor. She had nudged him onto the tracks in front of a train. They had called it suicide. *Now, his misery is over.*

She pushed to her feet and took off her nightgown. After her shower, she dressed in a navy blue suit, adding a shoulder holster to her left side. She tucked a gun in then strapped a Glock 26 to the inside of her thigh. She pulled her jacket on, making sure to hide the bulge of the firearm before grabbing her car keys. The door automatically locked behind her.

When she got to the car, she double-checked to make sure both weapons were loaded and ready to go. As she approached Georgetown, her phone rang. She flipped on the headset.

"What's up, Sumner?"

"I'm looking for that report on the Beirut incident. Did you keep a copy?"

"It's either on my desk or in the files under Eden Wyatt. Why do you need it?"

"Justice department has a couple of questions about Blake. Seems like he's telling tales about Eden."

"Those aren't tales. We know they're true."

"I know. But I prefer to handle these kind of messes in my department by myself. I don't need them butting in."

"Relax, Sumner. I'll send them something when I get back."

"You're coming back to the office after we...uh, close this situation?"

"Damn right. No reason to miss work. We've got a ton to do. The paperwork on her termination will take me a week to fill out." She chuckled. *And I'll love every minute of it.*

"I leave that up to you. Got another call. Justice department again. Damn, fucking bastards. See you soon." She removed her headset at the next red light. When it turned green, she took a right onto Key Bridge to cross over into Virginia.

* * * *

When Eden arrived at the warehouse, hers was the only car there. She smiled to herself at the stealth of her team. *Bless their little hearts.* She took a breath, straightened her jacket, patted her holster, and walked toward the building. As she approached, she noticed several broken windows. *Rocks thrown by bored teenagers?*

Memories of cold, lonesome nights spent on that thin cot, huddled under the one ratty blanket, returned. *Some safe house. Safe from terrorists, but not from rats.* Broken glass at the main entrance drew her eye. *Is this crap or put here to divert me to another entrance? Don't be paranoid. Paranoia gets people killed.*

A small shudder rocketed up her spine as she opened the door. *The goddamn, creaking, old door will tell the whole state what I'm doing. Geez.* As she pushed it open the noise grew louder then stopped. A glance told her the hinges were rusty.

The gargantuan room was lit only by afternoon sun. It was dark, and shadowy. She reached for a light and got her fingers caught in a sticky spider web. She jumped at the eerie feeling then stepped back and let her eyes adjust. Within a few minutes, she was able to see the switch. Gingerly, she reached over and flipped it, but nothing happened. *Figures.*

She was early. Sumner and Lynn weren't supposed to arrive for twenty minutes. Eden suspected the men and Tara were already in place. She sat on a rickety folding chair by the card table and touched her thigh. Blake's phone was in her pants pocket. The mic was in her jacket and there was one disguised as an earring, too.

Twenty minutes later, a black Lincoln Town Car pulled up. Eden went to the window, climbing on a crate far enough back so as not to be seen. After a few heart-pounding seconds, the driver's door opened, and Sumner stepped out. He looked around and headed toward the door. On the threshold, he paused a second and took a deep breath, before turning the knob to enter.

"Hello, Sumner," Eden said as he stepped in. She frowned upon seeing him, sad to think he might be part of this nasty plot. The old feelings she'd once had had morphed into a sort of friendship. The suspicion that he might be the traitor caused a conflict within her. The hope of his innocence tugged hard on her heart.

He patted his side before replying. "So, you've got the phone?"

Eden noticed the slight bulge of a gun under his arm. Adrenaline pumped through her veins. "I do."

The door opened again, and Lynn walked in. "I see you found the traitor."

"What? Me?" Eden's eyes went wide, and she gestured to her own chest.

"Yes, you. You betrayed Jerry. Had him killed then faked your capture. We know everything."

Eden couldn't believe what she was hearing. Anger swelled up in her at the lies. *Is Sumner buying this bullshit?* A bead of sweat formed on her brow as she shifted from foot to foot.

She looked at Sumner, who returned her gaze. She saw anger and betrayal on his face.

"Sumner, you have to believe it wasn't me," Eden pleaded.

"We know it's you," Lynn replied. "We have all the evidence."

Sumner stared at Eden.

"You're the traitor, Lynn. I can prove it."

"Let's settle all this at the office. Give me the phone," Sumner said, as he moved toward Eden.

"Stay away from me. I'm not the traitor."

Two consecutive gunshots rang out, and Sumner fell to the ground. Eden stood with her mouth agape. Lynn smiled. She turned to Eden and spoke, "Now, it's your turn, girlie."

"Why?"

"You're the reason Rosemary is dead. She killed herself because Jerry left her for you—a disgusting little whore. Sumner didn't have the guts to shoot you, but I do. I'm relieving him of the responsibility."

"You killed Sumner and now me? What's your plan? You can't escape. They'll catch you."

"Not if I make it look like a murder-suicide. You killed Sumner because he was going to turn you in. Then, you realized you couldn't get away with it, so you killed yourself. The cops'll figure it that way when they find the evidence I'm leaving."

"Evidence?"

"The emails and letters prove you killed Sumner and betrayed Jerry."

Eden looked at her, confused.

"It's the power of computers, girl. I can make anything look like you sent it."

"How will this bring back Rosemary?" Eden slid her fingers to her holster.

"It won't. But it'll punish the one, last, remaining guilty party—you." Lynn slapped Eden's hand, pushing it away from the weapon. Then, she raised her pistol and aimed it at Eden's chest.

A shot rang from the balcony—Mick's sniper rifle. Lynn fell over.

Eden rushed to Sumner, kneeling next to him, checking for a pulse. A groan indicated that he was still alive. She saw the bulletproof vest underneath his jacket.

"Hold still." Eden pulled out her cell.

"Put the phone down," Sumner said in a tight voice. He rolled to his right side and propped himself up. "Hurts like hell. Probably a broken rib." Pulling out his gun, he held it to Eden's chest.

Her eyes widened. "I didn't shoot you."

A shot rang out from the doorway, striking Sumner in the arm. He dropped the Glock, and Eden picked it up. Tom ran in, keeping his weapon trained on Sumner while he kicked the gun away from Lynn's body. He bent down to check her pulse.

Sumner gripped his arm to stem the flow of blood. "Then who did?"

"Lynn." Eden nodded toward the body lying still on the floor.

"She's gone," Tom said.

Mick stood up, crouching in the loft because of the low ceiling.

"Lynn shot me? Why?" Sumner looked at Eden. "I thought she loved me."

Eden patted his shoulder. "Lynn didn't love anybody. Except Rosemary."

"You're a traitor. I have to take you in."

"Lynn lied."

"She had evidence."

"Falsified. I've never been a traitor. I thought you knew me better than to believe that."

"I thought I knew Lynn, too."

"She used you."

"Thanks for pointing out the obvious." Sumner stared into Eden's eyes. "I didn't want to believe that about you. But she was very convincing."

By this time, Mick had joined them from the loft. He dialed. "Gotta tell Tara Eden's okay."

"I have to call an ambulance, Sumner," Eden said.

"I'm okay."

"No, you're not." *Can't believe I still feel something for him, even though he tried to shoot me.*

His face grew pale, and he inched over to lean against a wall.

"Sumner, you don't look good."

"Another compliment. You're killing me with all this sweet talk."

Eden shot him a rueful smile as she spoke to 911. When she hung up, she took his hand.

"We were once lovers. Who'd have thought we'd end up like this?" Sumner whispered.

Eden cupped his cheek. "You sent the Marines for me in Beirut, didn't you?"

He nodded. "Evidence be damned. You were still my agent. I couldn't let you die."

She leaned over and kissed his cheek. Tom cleared his throat. Eden glanced over at him. His face appeared a bit flushed. Before she could speak, the sound of a siren in the distance drew their attention.

"Can you stand?" Eden asked Sumner.

"I think so."

Tom shouldered Eden out of the way and yanked Sumner up on shaky legs. He wobbled a bit before Mick caught him on the other side.

"Mick. Eden. Tom. You guys okay?" A female voice followed the slam of a car door. Tara joined her husband.

Tom and Mick propped Sumner against the wall. Tara snaked her arm around Mick's waist and lifted her chin. Mick shouldered his rifle and kissed his wife.

Tom pulled Eden in close. She raised her gaze to his. "Thank you." Tom lowered his mouth to press against hers. She softened in his embrace.

"Oh, it's like that?" Sumner asked.

Eden broke from Tom. "Yeah. Sumner, let me introduce you to Tom Davis. He's the Marine you sent in to rescue me."

"He's a fast worker. You ready for another assignment?" Sumner asked, as the siren got louder and finally stopped.

"Yep. As Mrs. Tom Davis. I'm quitting the CIA," Eden announced.

Sumner shot a half smile her way as the EMT's approached.

"Who's injured here?" one asked Mick, who pointed to the man in the suit.

"I don't blame you. I'll miss you." Summer grimaced in pain.

"It's time. Time for me to move on."

Tom squeezed her shoulders and smiled.

"Better call the coroner," Mick said to the man taking Sumner's pulse.

"Oh? A body?"

Mick indicated Lynn on the ground, behind a crate.

"Damn. I see." The man picked up his radio and called it in.

The second EMT eased Sumner down on the stretcher.

"Tell the cops to call me. I'll straighten this out," Sumner said as the two sturdy men rolled him toward the ambulance.

"Will do. Take care."

"You, too, Eden. Stay in touch."

Eden's heart swelled as she watched them roll away the man who had held her life in his hands. Tom slipped his arm around her waist. She looked up at him and grinned. *Now, he's my life.*

Relief and happiness flooded her veins, making her almost high. Another siren wailed, signaling the arrival of the police. Mick and Tara dusted off some chairs. When the cops entered, they approached Tom first.

"Who's in charge here?"

"I am. Lt. Colonel Davis." He shook hands with the two policemen.

"Dead body?" One officer cocked an eyebrow.

"The coroner's already been called."

"Bucking for my job?" he joked.

Tom laughed. "I've got enough on my plate."

The cop eyed Eden and nodded. "I'd say so."

Chapter Fifteen

Two days later, in St. Thomas.

    Tara put a large pitcher of margaritas and four tumblers on the table on the deck. Mick and the others carried out guacamole, chips, salsa, and two kinds of dip. Tom pulled Eden into his lap as Tara filled the glasses. Mick straddled a chair, his gaze sliding down his wife's body slowly.
    "I can't believe it's over." Eden gave a slight shake of her head.
    "That was close," Mick said, taking a sip. "Lynn almost took you out."
    "Quick reflexes, Mick." Eden raised her glass to him.
    "I'm glad everyone is okay. This scared the crap out of me," Tara said.
    "It wasn't a picnic. Sumner totally surprised me." Tom took a drink.
    "Me, too. Thank God you were ready," Eden said.
    "Now you can get on with your life, Eden. So, what's your plan?" Tara dipped a chip in the salsa.
    "Well—"
    But before she could speak, Tom took a small, velvet box out of his pocket. He opened it and slipped the engagement ring resting there on Eden's finger. "How about this, first?" He kissed her.
    Eden laughed. "I guess it's time to live. Really live. Freely. Like other people."
    "You're safe," Mick said, raising his glass. "Let's toast to a new life, a better life, for Eden and Tom."
    After they drained the liquid, Tara poured refills.
    "North Carolina?" Eden cocked an eyebrow at Tom.
    "Yep."
    "I think there might be a house for sale near the one we own," Mick said.
    "Then, we wouldn't have to break this group up," Eden replied. "Wedding on the beach?"

"Whatever you want, beautiful."

"Here? Can I help plan?" Tara wiggled in her chair. Mick laughed.

"I was hoping you'd volunteer, because I don't know crap about weddings and parties and stuff." Eden sipped her margarita.

"Mick and I got married here, too."

"Perfect," Tom said. "There's no place more beautiful to tie the knot."

At the end of the week, Tom returned to the States to go back to his command. Eden and Tara jumped into planning with glee. Tara dragged her friend to every island woman who sewed, looking for just the right dress.

Tara's mother flew down, helped them plan a menu, and invited about twenty guests. Days flew by so quickly, Eden couldn't keep track. A smile never left her face as she looked toward a future filled with happiness instead of uncertainty, filled with love instead of fear.

She began the long road back from Post-Traumatic Stress Disorder to normal life by spending an hour a week with a therapist and teaching herself to sleep without a gun under her pillow. For the first time, she dreamt about children and a house she could share with Tom. Her nightmares began to fade, happening less frequently.

Eden lost herself in phone calls to her grandmother, who had saved her the first time. They laughed and planned the service. Gram was anxious to meet Tom and figure out if he deserved her precious girl.

Tom scouted out small houses and apartments in Jacksonville, North Carolina. Eden gave him the green light to rent the place he liked best that they could afford on his salary alone. He found the ideal quarters and put down a deposit. Eden could live there, near Mick and Tara, while Tom served out the rest of his obligatory time on assignment in Georgia. He planned to travel home to her on weekends.

He emailed pictures, making Eden's mouth water, soon to be living there with him. She loved the location. The house was small, but there was space for a garden on one side. She began researching the types of vegetables and flowers she could plant there.

"I never thought of you as a gardener," Tara said.

"You'd be surprised. I can sew, too. Gram didn't miss a trick."

"You're gonna scare the hell outta Tom." Mick took a gulp of his beer.

"Why?"

"He thought he was marrying a tough operative, not a domestic goddess."

"Domestic goddess? You're kidding?"

"Yep." He grinned.

"Hey. I hope I won't be sitting around all day, waiting for him to get home. I'll be working."

"Working?" Tara raised her eyebrows.

"I've got a few things brewing."

"Oh boy. This is gonna be some surprise." Mick shook his head.

Eden laughed. "I'm resourceful."

Tara poured another glass of iced tea. "I bet you are."

"You have to make your own opportunities in this world."

"I agree. Like us turning being stranded on a deserted island into a sexy vacation for tourists."

"That was brilliant," Eden agreed.

"And every once in a while, we camp out there, too. Just to check on things," Tara said.

"Bullshit. We camp out there to—"

"Mick!"

"Okay, okay." He raised his hands. "I won't spill the beans. But Eden's got an imagination, I'm sure she's figured it out." He snickered.

"I love you two. The flame never dies, does it?" Eden asked.

"Not if I can help it," Mick muttered.

* * * *

The day was perfect for a wedding—clear sky and eighty-two degrees. In the guest bedroom, Tara, her mother, and Eden's grandmother fussed over Eden. She wore a simple dress made out of white cotton piqué. The strapless gown was full length, tucked in at the waist, and had a skirt that was narrow at the hip but fuller at the ankle.

Her blonde hair hadn't totally grown in, but it almost reached her shoulders, allowing Gram to make a fancy do with white roses. A simple strand of pearls around her neck with matching earrings from her grandmother was something old.

The flowers in her hair were new. The panties she wore were light blue, and her gold bracelet was borrowed from Tara's mom. Backless, white sandals with faux pearls were necessary, as she'd be walking through sand. Nerves gripped her stomach.

She peeked out the window and spied Tom pacing slowly with a drink in his hand. She gasped to see how handsome he looked. When he glanced her way, she let the curtain fall back into place so he wouldn't see her. She laughed, knowing he'd caught sight of the moving drapery and knew she'd been staring at him.

Tom was standing in his full evening dress "A" uniform. It was the one he donned only during the most formal occasions. He wore an evening coat with sleeve ornamentation, strip collar, white waistcoat, and white shirt with pique placket. The midnight blue trousers sported a thin, red stripe inside of a gold embroidered one. All of his medals and ribbons were prominently displayed on his right chest, making an impressive sight.

Before she could have a full-fledged panic attack, the music sounded. Everyone cleared out except Eden and her grandmother, who was to give her away. Gram took a deep breath.

"Your parents would have been so proud. Grandpa too. You're an exceptional young woman, Eden, and I couldn't be more proud of you. I love you with all my heart. Now, it's time to join you with that fine, young man. Let's go. Don't want you to totally fall apart before the 'I do's' are said." She chuckled.

Taking Gram's hand, Eden followed her outside. The ceremony was to take place under the shade of a tiny grove of coconut trees. The justice of the peace stood in front of Mick and Tom. When the guitar stopped, the men turned around. Tom gasped aloud when he saw Eden, making her smile. She took a calming breath and walked down the aisle, gripping Gram's arm.

When her gaze met Tom's, all her nerves fluttered away like a butterfly in the wind. A peace flowed through her, and she knew in her heart she was doing the right thing.

"Who gives this woman?" The magistrate asked.

"Her mother, her father, and her grandfather, may their souls rest in peace, and I do."

Eden and her grandmother embraced. Gram wiped a tear from her cheek. Eden's eyes were full.

The Lt. Colonel took her from Gram and laced her fingers with his. Together they faced the man who would join them for life.

After they said the vows, Tom shoved the ring on her finger with a bit too much force, causing the audience to titter. Color suffused his cheeks.

"*Psst*. They get it. I'm yours. You can relax now," she whispered.

He grinned down at her. The man conducting the service took off his glasses and cleared his throat.

The couple faced forward, their smiles melting.

When it was Eden's turn, her hand trembled slightly as she slipped the band on Tom's finger.

He chuckled and their gazes met. "It's not too late to run for the hills," he said, leaning over to deliver his words to her ears only.

"Not letting you off that easy, Davis," she replied, stifling a giggle.

The rest of the ceremony was quick, but the reception went on for several hours. Eating, drinking, singing, and dancing added to the joyousness of the occasion. Steel drum music put the bride in the arms of the groom. They waltzed together, their gazes locked, reminding Eden of their first dance on New Year's Eve in New York City.

Genuine happiness shone through her eyes at her husband. The rustle of the palm fronds in the background whispered that her time in the paradise that was St. Thomas would soon come to an end. But Eden knew that her nirvana with Tom Davis would last a lifetime.

By ten o'clock, Tom and Eden had changed and were ready to go to The Island Utopia Hotel for their wedding night.

Mick stopped them with his palm. "A fax came for you during the ceremony. I thought it might be important." He handed a paper to Eden.

"A fax?" Tom gave her a blank stare.

"Oh, yes." She nodded as she read.

Her new husband looked perplexed. "What's up?"

"You said you don't care if I work, right?"

"Hell, no. I'd never expect you to sit around all day." Tom slipped his arm around her waist.

"Good. Because this is a job offer from Carver Security."

"Carver Security?" Mick asked.

"Yep. In Jacksonville. They want me to start in two weeks."

Tom raised his eyebrows. "Security?"

"Isn't that dangerous?" Tara asked, mimicking his expression.

"Not for most people. But we're talking about my wife, here." Tom chuckled.

"I love you, too, Davis." She whipped out her phone and sent a text. "I accepted the job."

The End

About the Authors

Jean Joachim is a best-selling romance fiction author, with books hitting the Amazon Top 100 list since 2012. She was chosen Author of the Year in 2012 by the New York City chapter of Romance Writers of America. Her novel, *The Renovated Heart*, was chosen Best Novel of 2012 by Love Romances Café. *Lovers & Liars* was a finalist for Best Novel of 2013 by Love Romances Café. Her series, Hollywood Hearts was a finalist for Best Series of 2013 and Megan Davis and Chaz Duncan (from If I Loved You) finaled as Best Couple, 2013 by Love Romances Café. *The Marriage List* tied for third place from Gulf Coast RWA Chapter and, most recently, *Lovers & Liars* was selected as a 2013 Reader's Crown Finalist in Contemporary Romance by RomCon. Jean has 26 works of fiction published. Married and a mother of two sons, she lives in New York City with her family and a rescued pug named Homer.

Connect with Jean through email: sunnydaysbook@gmail, her blog: http://jeanjoachim.blogspot.com or her website: http://www.jeanjoachimbooks.com She'd love to hear from you.

Ben Tanner lives outside Atlanta with his wife, Denise, and their cat. A retired Marine, Ben served as a 2531-Field Radio Operator, Marine 2nd Force Reconnaissance 1991-1996, 4th LAAD 1996-1998. Although he has one and sometimes two day jobs, Ben is a writer at heart.

OTHER BOOKS BY SECRET CRAVINGS PUBLISHING

LOST & FOUND SERIES
With Benjamin Tanner
LOVE, LOST AND FOUND

MANHATTAN DINNER CLUB SERIES
RESCUE MY HEART
SEDUCING HIS HEART
SHINE YOUR LOVE ON ME
TO LOVE OR NOT TO LOVE

HOLLYWOOD HEARTS SERIES
IF I LOVED YOU
RED CARPET ROMANCE
MEMORIES OF LOVE
MOVIE LOVERS
LOVE'S LAST CHANCE
LOVERS & LIARS
HIS LEADING LADY (Series Starter)

NOW AND FOREVER SERIES
NOW AND FOREVER 1, A LOVE STORY
NOW AND FOREVER 2, THE BOOK OF DANNY
NOW AND FOREVER 3, BLIND LOVE
NOW AND FOREVER 4, THE RENOVATED HEART
N0W AND FOREVER 5, LOVE'S JOURNEY
NOW AND FOREVER, CALLIE'S STORY (series starter)

MOONLIGHT SERIES
UNDER THE MIDNIGHT MOON

Secret Cravings Publishing
www.secretcravingspublishing.com

Made in the USA
Lexington, KY
08 April 2015